Rosetta Stones

by Catherine Parra Dix

Published by Central Ave. Press

Requests to make copies of any part of the work should be mailed to the following address: Central Ave. Press 2132-A Central SE #144 Albuquerque, NM 87106

ISBN 13: 978-0-9798452-2-2

Library of Congress Cataloging-in-Publication Data

Dix, Catherine R. (Catherine Renee), 1971-
Rosetta stones / by Catherine R. Dix.
    p. cm.
Summary: Just before they are to graduate from their Santa Ana, New Mexico high school, close friends Antonia, Joey, Javen, and Sonny witness a terrifying crime, and Antonia finally uncovers the truth about the nightmares that have haunted her for as long as she can remember.
    ISBN 978-0-9798452-2-2
    [1. Secrets--Fiction. 2. Murder--Fiction. 3. Friendship--Fiction. 4. Emotional problems--Fiction. 5. Mexican Americans--Fiction. 6. New Mexico--Fiction.] I. Title.

    PZ7.D6402Ro 2008
    [Fic]--dc22

                                                                2007032017

Book cover and design by Jennifer Chevais

Central Ave. Press
2132-A Central SE #144, Albuquerque, NM 87106
www.centralavepress.com

"It is queer how all in a minute you can understand what growing up means."

~author Noel Streatfield in *Theater Shoes*

Contents

Chapter 1
Antonia's Story

No one could possibly know how excited I was! It was Senior Ditch Day, and I sat on my hands, trying hard not to fidget, trying hard not to sing too loudly as I looked back at the long chain of borrowed cars and beat-up trucks following behind us that early Friday morning.

I rode in the back seat of my graduation gift, a brand new SUV Hybrid, the lead vehicle in this convoy. Javen took the wheel because he said he knew where we were going. It was more than the rest of us could say. I might not have been so accommodating if I hadn't wanted to revel in my excitement, without having to worry about road conditions or inconspicuous highway patrolmen anxious to meet their end-of-the-month quotas. Of course, this decision pleased Javen plenty. And when Javen was pleased, life was a lot easier for the rest of us.

He, Joey and Sonny were practically co-owners of my new "Suvee." I had brought them along to help me handpick what I'd be tooling around in after graduation. We all were in agreement about the hybrid, even if it was for completely different reasons. The guys liked the fact that it was an all-wheel-drive with a "kick-ass engine" and top-of-the-line CD player equipped with satellite radio. At the dealership, my wannabe-men slobbered over the conglomeration of metal beneath its hood as though it were a *Sports Illustrated* cover model, arguing over what shade of tint to apply and which rims to install on those sleek, black tires of mine. I let them. Weirder, though, *Mom* let them.

I liked the Suvee for three simple reasons: one, it was a hybrid, two, it was red, and three, it was roomy enough for all four of us. We were all pretty tired of cramming into Joey's truck.

Before now, Joey had been the only one lucky enough to own a vehicle. His was a ten-year-old Toyota pickup he'd saved up for and bought from Jackson's used car lot. He called it Pride. But Joey was very humble because Pride got him nowhere fast. It couldn't go over thirty miles per hour, which was just fine for cruising up and down main street, but shitty when we were running late in the morning. On the front bumper was a vanity plate that read: *Pride and Joey*. The standard wooden rosary given to confirmation candidates hung from his rearview mirror, and a wallet-sized, laminated picture of Saint Christopher was tucked into the plastic glass panel, slightly blocking his view of the speedometer.

After summer was over, Joey would be leaving us to attend Texas A&M. The rest of us would be New Mexico Staters. So far, it didn't sound as though Javen or Sonny (much less their parents) had any plans to buy a vehicle. Sonny's parents couldn't afford a car for the eldest of their five, and neither could he because his healthy appetite devoured everything he made working the evening shift at Arby's. Javen's parents, on the other hand, could easily afford it, but...well, they'd quit supporting him a year ago.

Needless to say, the Suvee was appreciated by all of us. This would be the day we officially broke it in. Already, after a mere two weeks of ownership, the interior seemed to be losing its new smell, now jumbled with the scent of Doritos and sunscreen, freshly showered bodies and Jack Daniels from the guys' early-morning shot.

This was my graduating class' last day together before the big event. Our last day to break loose, break the rules, maybe even break some minor laws. Somebody was bound to break a leg, break up or break down. One thing was for sure, though, we would brake for no one on our way to the hot springs. No one except Sonny, who already needed to take a whiz not even thirty-five minutes outside of town. The engine paused just long enough to fill the fresh air with a smorgasbord of music as we waited on him. I could pick up a little bit of honky-tonk country, Spanish laments, and angry rappers rumbling somewhere off in the distance, just before Javen rolled down the window and took a big whiff.

"Smells like teen spirit," he said before sliding Nirvana into the CD player. Kurt Cobain's incantation began drowning out everything else. Classic alt rock was always our musical choice, but this song just so happened to be the perfect selection for Senior Ditch Day, a long-held tradition that every parent in Santa Ana, New Mexico pretended not to know about. Even the superintendent. Of course, the superintendent also happened to be my mother. But what could she do the year her eldest daughter was graduating? Well, if she ever wanted me to speak to her again, she'd ignore it right along with everyone else's parents. It took three months and a little help from my friends to convince her that it was harmless and innocent and my last request as her soon-to-be-free captive. Mom never would've raised her white flag if it hadn't been for Joey's pragmatism, Sonny's boy-like charm, and Javen's perseverance. She gave a confirmed yes a whole two days before the big day. I was tempted to have her put it in writing.

Growing up in our town, children trick-or-treated like the Peanuts gang — in small, parentless groups. Not Madrid and me. Ours was the only mother who was never more than a foot away. *Overprotective* was too mild a word to describe her peculiarity. She was a woman who never let her daughters go to summer camps or anywhere else that required an overnight stay. My mom accompanied me on my first date and made me come home at 11:00 on prom night. This past New Year's Eve was the first time she'd allowed Madrid and me to stay out just past midnight, because Joey's parents were having a New Year's Eve/20th

Anniversary party, and she seemed to trust his parents like nobody else's. New Year's Eve was never fun around my mother, anyway. She slept a lot, cried a lot, ate a lot and spoke hardly at all. It used to worry me, make me just as depressed. Over time, we learned to expect it and just left her alone while trying hard not to take it personally.

But today, she had nothing to worry about because, although I definitely felt intoxicated, it wasn't from alcohol. I was high on the moonshine of freedom. My mother's love, as beautiful as it was, had always been suffocating.

But she was finally learning to relax a little. She was letting Madrid spend the night with her best friend Ashlin. And she was letting me spend the night with the rest of the Senior class out in the middle of nowhere. This was huge. I couldn't contain myself any longer. I turned to Joey and kissed him, solidly and unexpectedly.

"What was that for?" he asked after an awkward moment of silence. It surprised even me.

"Because we're graduating, Joey!" I finally said.

He looked confused. And I obviously looked embarrassed because his whole expression immediately changed. "Hey, you can kiss me anytime you want."

The mere fact that he realized I was embarrassed and tried to fix it meant everything to me. But the paradox of our relationship was this: He knew me well enough to know I was embarrassed, but hadn't a clue as to why.

"Hurry the hell up, Santino! We're burnin' daylight!" Javen shouted from up front, laying on my horn. Sonny zipped up and hopped back into the passenger seat; Javen put the Suvee in gear and we all began singing along with Kurt as we continued our journey up Highway 180.

Santa Ana was more than a couple of hours away from the springs. But it wasn't long before we reached Silver City. The flat rangeland slowly mutated into low hills scattered with more juniper and less creosote. Rock formations became more prominent the farther north we drove, leaving little room for cactus or cattle as the straight road we'd been following began to meander. I rolled down my window to inhale the cool mountain air and get a better view of the fast-moving trees. But those were hard to see with Javen's driving. So I turned my attention back to Joey, who was now diligently scribbling words I couldn't read into his notebook. If I didn't know him so well, my insides would be churning as I wondered what he was writing about so fervently. My breath? My chapped lips? My audacity? But I *did* know him so well. And he wasn't a journaler. Even if he decided to record the details of my kiss on paper, he would never be so obvious about it.

Joey. How does he put up with me? Today, it's poor attempts at spontaneity, and tomorrow...tomorrow was too far away to care about. I was too busy tracing his lips and caressing his skin with my eyes to care about tomorrow. I recited the second stanza of e.e. Cummings' poem *somewhere i have never travelled* to him — mentally, of course:

> *your slightest look easily will unclose me*
> *though i have closed myself as fingers,*
> *you open always petal by petal myself as Spring opens*
> *(touching skillfully, mysteriously) her first rose*

Today would be the day that I would finally announce this lyrical portrait of my feelings that I'd heard for the first time in Ms. McIntire's English class my junior year. I remember that, as she'd read it aloud, I closed my eyes and concentrated on someone in particular....

But before long, I was thinking of somebody else.

That was the day I realized with absolute certainty that what I felt for Joey was more than just friendship, and that what I felt for Javen was nothing more than that.

Joey was my first real memory.

I remember, after Mom walked me into my classroom at the Tiny Tots Learning Center, she kissed my cool three, maybe four-year-old forehead, whispered "I love you" into my ear, then hugged me as though she would never see me again. She slowly backed away, and I saw that she was crying. I couldn't remember ever feeling so afraid of the distance between us.

"I'll see you in a few hours, okay, mi'ja?" She tried to say it as normally as possible, just before turning to make a quick exit. There was no backward glance, no peek back into my room, no change of heart. She was gone, and I didn't know the difference between four minutes, four hours, or forever. All I knew was that catching her contagious tears was not an option for me. So I held my breath and shut my eyes tight in an effort not to draw attention to myself or confront the roomful of unfamiliar faces surely staring at me. I stood with my feet firmly planted next to the door, when the day care lady asked me to take her hand. *Take my hand. Take my hand,* she repeated. I think her name was Miss Baeza. After a few moments, my thoughts shifted from the fear of crying to a yearning to exhale.

I couldn't. I wouldn't! But the lady's voice was growing angrier and angrier with each request to take her stupid hand. And just as I felt I couldn't take any more, there was a soft, warm little hand interlocking fingers with mine. I blew out the air in my lungs and opened my eyes. A warm tear fell onto our clasped hands. The little boy standing in front of me smiled and said, "We catched it jus' in time before it heated the floor."

"Heated?" I repeated.

"No." He said the word slower and louder. "Heeeated." I realized he meant *hitted. Hit,* actually.

He was a skinny little boy with curly black hair, glasses and a wide smile. He didn't speak English very well, but I understood him perfectly; he was being kind. "Come on. It's okay. I weal help you," he said. I thought about how his voice was even softer than his hands as he led me around the room and introduced me to his friends: Javen Schroeder, Santino Goretti, Eddie Fuentes, Tommy Akin, and Dolores Teran. He squeezed my sweaty hand all the while. Joey Diaz would become my very best friend. e.e. Cummings made me confront the possibility that I might lose him forever after we graduated. He also made me realize that Joey knew me better than anyone else in the whole world.

My feelings for him may never have evolved had it not been for his own gradual evolution. Gone were the chunky glasses in the ninth grade; I think he grew six inches the following year. By our junior year, he was tall; he was strong; he was...around me way too much! I knew each pair of his Wranglers by heart and was especially fond of the ones with the torn left back pocket, perfectly rundown.

Still, the best part about Joey was his hands, as warm as worked clay and, I'd swear, intuitive. They knew exactly when I needed my neck rubbed, instinctively reached for mine when they sensed I was frightened or nervous, offered to carry my heavy backpack before my lips had the chance to ask, and recognized when my body needed to be hugged or touched in a way that kept two friends connected on a level that can only be described as sacred.

If only he knew these things. If only I knew how he felt. In all these years, he'd never given me the slightest indication that he wanted more than just a friendship. Of course, touching my hair, holding my hand — those things could be construed as flirting. But his eyes never showed me what I needed to see. His lips never said what I needed to hear, and they never ever came close to mine, except for a few moments ago when I took the initiative and kissed him. And then the reality of it finally hit me. I just kissed *Joey* for the first time in my life. And it was so meaningless! So fast and completely unromantic. I suddenly felt sick to my stomach.

This was supposed to be the day I made my feelings known. Was it too late? Did I ruin things so early in the day with that silly kiss? He didn't have a girlfriend, but what if this was the day he decided to hook up with someone?

Every senior girl would be there, not to mention all those underclass girls who would find their way over —

"All right, so what's the plan for any underclassmen brave enough to show?" Sonny asked, interrupting my thoughts. Or reading them.

"There's no plan," Javen said. "If they're on this caravan, their ass is grass. They had fair warning already."

"Are you going to object to any of the underclass girls partying with us?" I facetiously asked, secretly hoping for a yes.

He laughed. "Only if they're ugly."

I snorted in disgust.

"Hey, why don't you make yourself useful and get me a beer?" he shouted back to me.

"Because, number one, if I wanted to be useful today, I'd be driving. And number two, there's no drinking while you're driving the Suvee."

"Gimme a break, Miss Goody-Two-Shoes. I've already drank."

"All right, Jav, I wasn't going to count your morning shot of whiskey, but if you insist...."

"Even if it did count, it was enough for you, Buddy. You're driving," Joey chimed in.

"One beer isn't gonna do anything but quench my thirst and you know it, kiss-ass." Javen just didn't know when to quit.

"I'll take that beer!" Sonny shouted.

I glared at him to show my disapproval.

"Hey, I'm not the one drivin'!"

Joey opened the cooler from in back and tossed a can to Sonny.

"It's nine-thirty in the friggin' morning. I can't believe you guys can't wait 'til after lunch," he said.

"It was eight in the friggin' morning when —"

"Conversation over, Javen. Get over it and change the CD already," I interrupted. I didn't know what was more annoying, his speeding and swerving or his persistence to drink.

Then Javen slowed down almost to a stop and rolled down his window. "Give me your can, Sonny."

"Screw you, Man. I'm not letting you toss out a good beer."

"Just give me the can!"

Sonny hissed a few cusswords before returning to his over-obliging self who did whatever Javen wanted him to do. Once he'd pulled to the side of the road, Javen lowered the music and hung the beer in his left hand out the open window. Footsteps approached. We turned to see a breathless hitchhiker running toward us. He was a middle-aged man wearing a tie-dyed t-shirt, long, thick dreadlocks, a grizzled beard, and a backpack that looked older than he did.

"What are you doing, Javen?" I asked, starting to panic, especially when I saw the way that his cat-like eyes were penetrating the hitchhiker as though he were his prey. Javen's face intensified as the hitchhiker's face relaxed, smiling at Javen trustfully, slowing his pace as he approached the driver's side window. I felt that old familiar fear. Not of the hitchhiker, but of unpredictable, uncontrollable, oftentimes unstoppable Javen. And yet, despite my primed panic, I was still completely unprepared for what he was about to do.

"You need a lift, Buddy?"

The hitchhiker wiped beads of sweat from his brow and tried to catch his breath just long enough to speak. "Yeah. Thanks," he managed.

I looked into his kind eyes, wishing Javen had never stopped. He was just a man, a tired man who needed a ride somewhere. But we were on a mission. Before I could complete my next thought, Javen violently shook the can of beer in his hand, popped it open, and threw it at the hitchhiker.

"This should cool you off 'til you get one," he said. And we were off.

He hammered the gas and waved his arm out the window, signaling the cars behind us to keep going. Joey and I both looked back at the man left standing in the road, now soaked in cheap beer. We sat in silence and utter disgust while Javen roared with laughter.

It was Joey who spoke first. "Dude, what the hell was that? I knew you were mean, and I knew you could be an ass, but that was...that was sick, Man!"

"Yeah, well, maybe you should'a just stayed home today, Buddy. We're on this trip to have some fun."

"You call that fun?" I asked. "That's it! I've had it with you! Pull over!"

"Oh, c'mon, Antonia, admit it. That was funny!"

"I said pull over!"

"What's the matter with you?"

"What's the matter with *me*?"

"She said pull over, Man. It's her car. Just do it."

"You stay out of this, Joey. Why are you always so quick to butt in?"

"Javen...."

"You, too, Sonny? Man, I cannot believe you guys. He was a fucking hitchhiker! It's not like you'll ever see him again."

"Javen, shut up and look!" Sonny said, pointing to the side of the road. There stood a middle-aged man wearing a tie-dyed shirt, long dreadlocks, and a grizzled beard. He wore a smile that wasn't soaked in cheap beer anymore, watching intently as we passed him in what felt like slow motion.

I screamed. Joey, Sonny, and Javen could do nothing more than stare in disbelief.

"No way. That *couldn't* have been the same guy," Javen finally said when no one else spoke up.

"Really? Who else would it be, Javen? How many guys have you met over the course of your entire life who look like that, much less in two minutes?" I yelled.

"I don't know!"

"He was laughing at you, Jav," Joey said sarcastically.

"Shut the fuck up, Joey!"

"Was that...a ghost?" Sonny asked. "Do you think everyone else saw that?"

"Dude, it wasn't a ghost."

"Well then how the hell else can you explain it? Nobody else could have picked him up and dropped him off so quick. Nobody even passed us. And do you think he could run up ahead faster than this car? Without us even noticing? I don't think so, Man." Sonny turned back to Joey. "Now I really do need a beer."

No one said another word about it, not even Javen. We stopped once more, this time at a convenience store in Glenwood. Javen washed my windshield, checked my tires, paid for some gas. And when I held open my hand for the keys, he put a bag of black licorice in it, my favorite.

"How did you know I wanted this?"

"I know you better than you think."

"Well then you must know that I want my keys now. So be a good, little asshole and head to the rear."

Surprisingly, he didn't argue. He just handed me the keys. Of course, he didn't go to the back. He went around and took Sonny's place in the passenger's seat.

We weren't even a few miles down the road when his guilt got the best of him. That or he grew tired of the silence.

"I fucked up. There, I said it, are you guys happy? I shouldn't have screwed around like that.

"But I still don't think it's anything to get so freaked over."

Still, no one said a word.

"You wanna hear my theory?" he continued. Nobody answered. Of course, that didn't stop him. "Okay, so here it is. They have to be twins playing a sick joke on people passing by. Just walking apart, making everyone think they're seeing a ghost. The only difference between us and everyone else who's passed them is that we were smart enough to screw them before they screwed us. Well...I was smart enough."

Joey laughed. "That's it? Your theory is that you out-smarted a couple of old farts who had nothing better to do with their time than to scare people out in the middle of nowhere?"

"Don't you think there's somethin' spooky about twins?" Sonny asked.

"Don't you mean something spooky about ghosts?" I asked back.

"Shit yeah. Them, too."

The conversation was dropped for the remainder of the drive. But I couldn't get that guy's face out of my head. He wasn't scary. In fact, when I pictured his face, I saw some-one kind. What was scary about him was the way he'd reappeared — and laughed. Come to think of it, he wasn't laughing. He was just grinning at us. He was just smiling. A million thoughts were whirling around in my mind about him. *What the hell happened back there? Who was that guy, and what did he want?* I felt nauseous. I really didn't want to drive, but I didn't want anyone else driving, either. I watched the road intently, waiting for the man to pop up again. He never did.

The next thing I knew we were driving into the camp-site, greeted by the outdoorsy aromas of lighter fluid, pine and mossy water. The air was filled with conversation and laughter, the Gila's rushing water and more good-times music.

Everyone had gone on ahead after Javen made his last stop in Glenwood. So by the time we reached the springs, Tommy Akin and Eddie Fuentes were already inner-tubing down the Gila River. Dolores Teran and her fellow cheer-leader friends were quick to find and claim the prime hang-out spot, an area with plenty of sunshine and viewing potential to display their school-colored bikinis. School spirit to the end, I supposed.

Most everyone else loitered around the campsite — hungry teens who couldn't wait much longer for the hamburgers, steaks, and hot dogs soon to be grilling atop the white-hot charcoals. Already, beer was being passed around from the kegs in the back of Eddie's truck. I heard someone say that the San Francisco springs were crowded with bums and old hippies. But for the time being, the fun was at camp where a bunch of girls were setting up a volleyball net or on the river where, like the pied piper, it led most of the boys with its musical current.

From the looks of things, no one else had seen or experienced anything out of the ordinary. It seemed almost ridiculous to bring up the hitchhiker without anyone else mentioning it first. Besides, I don't think any of us wanted to think about him anymore.

The boys started taking off their shirts as they made their way down to the river. Joey touched me on the shoulder. "What are you gonna do?" he asked.

"Hey, don't worry about me. I'm sure Dolores will let me hang out with them. If not, there's always volleyball," I said, motioning my head toward the game that had already started.

"*Let* you?"

"You know what I mean."

Joey hated when I made like I was unwanted and unpopular. I knew the very idea that those girls might reject me bothered him. I was regretting my choice of words and tried to make a quick save. "Quit worrying. It'll be fine. She *needs* my presence to make her feel beautiful amongst her cheerleader friends."

Unconvinced, he hesitated before saying, "All right. I'm gonna join these guys for a little while. I'll catch up with you a little later, okay?"

"Have fun."

He grabbed my hand and squeezed it. "You be careful."

"I will if you will," I said as I let go, walking away as quickly as possible.

I looked back to see if he was giving me a fatherly glower. He was. It eased my disappointment, if only momentarily.

I popped open the back of my Suvee, grabbed the bag of licorice Javen had bought me and stuffed it into my backpack with my iPod and journal.

What was I in the mood for? I didn't think I'd find anything under the heading of "Dampered Plans." But I did find something close. The Cranberries. It was their depressing, yet satisfying, *No Need to Argue* CD. Song number two, "I Can't Be With You", number four-"Zombie", number five,"Empty", number eight, "Disappointment", number nine, "Ridiculous Thoughts" — yes, this was definitely what I was looking for.

I walked to the hot springs alone. I couldn't have told Joey that I'd really *planned* to sit at the springs. He would've insisted on coming with me. Best friend or not, he would've been harassed for the rest of the day for choosing me over them. Especially today. Most of these guys would probably never hang out this way again. Eddie had gotten a football scholarship to play at University of Arizona. Tommy was going with him, albeit not to attend college. And then, of course, Joey was off to Texas A&M. This day was truly golden for them. I'd never really felt the need for a close girlfriend before now.

I followed the sandy trail on the side of the cliff overlooking the river. It easily accommodated two people walking side-by-side or hand-in-hand, about a ten-minute walk from camp. Then again, it probably just seemed wider and longer than normal because I was walking it alone. Ponderosa and piñón, douglas fir, blue spruce, and southwestern white pines grew more and more dense as I approached the springs, eventually blocking the view of the river altogether. I could still hear it rushing like an angry herd of buffalo.

I'd recently given an oral report on the ecology of the

Gila National Forest for biology class. The meat of it was so fresh in my head that I could still remember that the scent of a mature Ponderosa pine's bark is very similar to the scent of vanilla, and that the southwestern white pine oozes resin for a few days after cutting, so it doesn't make for a really good Christmas tree. I prided myself on knowing how to identify these different trees by their needles and cones, if only for the next few weeks, at which point my brain would spring a slow leak that would drain all that data right along with any other useless information I'd accumulated over the last few months. I'd always envied Joey for his ability to remember everything. I used to tell him that if he were a comic book superhero, he could call himself Memory Man.

For the moment, though, I knew the ups and downs of these beautiful trees, and studying them brought the hot spring pools into sight faster than I'd anticipated. I was slightly disappointed to find the circular, sandy area surrounding them much more crowded than I'd hoped. Thankfully, though, nobody looked like a bum or a hippy.

It was a Friday, and judging by the number of people already at the springs, everyone was getting a jump-start on their summer. I searched out a quiet place to sit as I walked past a couple of girls in lounge chairs who were reading magazines as they tanned in the late morning sun. Some older ladies were sprawled out on the ground like starfish, sprinkled with sand from turning over a time or two. Four younger kids were splashing around while their mother drank a soda and looked on. Her husband pretended to sleep, eyes camouflaged by dark sunglasses, his lawn chair facing all the action at the big pool.

The big pool was where most everyone I recognized sat; the water temperature was perfect, I heard someone say as I kept walking. *Perfect for what?* I wondered. *Washing dishes?* These were hot springs, after all. So it was a little strange to see that on the west side a couple of guys were jumping from an indention in the cliff probably ten feet off the ground, into a pool where the water reached probably eight feet deep. I laughed aloud at these boys showing off for the crowd of girls watching. Having all-male friends had taught me a thing or two about why they act the way they do. Although I couldn't imagine what would inspire a person to dive, like a vegetable spear, into hot water.

I decided that the best place for me was at the shallowest area of a small, unpopulated pool where the clear water could warm my ankles while I sat on its shores. I cracked open my thick, plum-colored journal with the ruled pages, a Christmas gift from Madrid. *Dream Journal* was printed on the front in gold. Inside, she'd written a note that said this was a place for me to make sense of my many dreams. It was a sweet gift. My sister knew my dreams ranged from the innocent to the horrific. She also knew they were plentiful and draining.

I always addressed my journal to my father, as though we were corresponding, only I addressed him by his first name. I wasn't familiar enough with him to use the word Dad. And I guess it wasn't corresponding in the truest sense; the communication was one-way. But since I currently had both the time and material, I pulled out the matching pen and began to write:

Dear Matthew,

It was a good-dream night. I dreamt of the little lady again, the one with the shaky English. She smiled that sly smile of hers, as if she had something in store for me. The little man was there, too. As usual, I couldn't understand what he was trying to say to me, but he did his best to make me laugh with his big eyes and goofy faces.

They gave me biscochos and hugs and let me wander their home again as if all the porcelain knick-knacks displayed on every flat surface were unbreakable.

I always see the house through a veil of antique yellow, inhaling a medley of smells — it's musty, lemony like furniture polish, with a hint of pan dulce and coffee wafting in from the kitchen. I feel so safe, welcomed. It's like coming home.

Instead of the usual small-talk, I asked the lady for answers. She said they are already with me, safely locked away. And then she said something I couldn't quite understand. She said, "Your hand holds the key; use it when you're ready."

Again, I don't know what it all means. But I'm recording it anyway, and maybe someday it will all become crystal clear.

As for today, it isn't turning out to be anything like I'd hoped. I had built up so much anticipation before we even left. I wore my lucky earrings. I said a prayer...I felt sure that today would be perfect. So much for perfect. I never expected to run into a ghost before Senior Ditch Day even started. (I'm still freaked out about that one.) And I certainly never expected to have the time to write to you. Please don't take this the wrong way, but I'd just brought you along for a sense of comfort. Maybe for an end-of-the-day report. I should've known the boys would all congregate for their last manly assemblage. I suppose I did know. But just between you and me, I had hoped that Joey would say, "I'd rather hang out with you today, Antonia."

Things can't get any worse, though, right? I do have time on my side... and you, of course.

Sometimes I sense Joey feels the same way I do, but what if I'm wrong?

I paused a long while, reading what I'd just written as that old, familiar aching in my chest tried to settle. I squirmed and fought it off, but it stung. It was hurting more than usual. *Just cry*, it said. *Just let me out and it will all be better. I promise to go away if you just let me out.*

"No!" I shouted. And then there was laughter around me. I looked up and saw a group of girls staring at me.

I quickly closed my journal and dug into my bag of licorice. But the girls just waded away without so much as a second glance.

It was time to tune out the world. I put on my earphones, clicked on The Cranberries, and continued to write where I'd left off:

All right, enough with the self-pity. I'm only drawing attention to myself.

It's already been established that I don't know how Joey feels. And you and I are both aware that I may never get any of those answers that the little old lady was referring to, the ones she claims I'm carrying with me as we speak. But from this point forward, I'm just going to concern myself with trying to have a good time. So wish me luck! And thanks for listening.

"Ode to My Family," song number one, finished playing. Good song. But I really didn't want to hear the Cranberries after all. I pressed Stop and took off my headphones.

"Nice penmanship," someone said from behind me.

I jerked around to get a better look at the owner of this cheeky, unfamiliar voice. A young guy claimed ownership — blond, tanned, obviously brimming with the kind of confidence it takes to get away with rudeness when it came to lonely-looking girls.

"I'm sorry. I didn't realize I was sharing this with a total stranger. Would you like to come and have a closer look?" I said sarcastically.

"I was just passing through. I glanced into your book and...I hope you know that I didn't actually read it. I guess it was the best way I could come up with to get you to turn around and smile, not look so sad. I'm sorry."

"Well now that I've turned around, maybe you can see that I'm not sad — or smiling for that matter." I was standing up by now, pulling my bag over my shoulder and dusting the sand off my backside.

"Please, don't leave. I didn't mean any harm, really. I'm just bad at this."

"Bad at what, getting someone to turn around and smile?"

"Well, there's that...conversation, actually. Just meeting people in general." He was fidgeting and nervously running his hand through that shiny, blonde hair.

I suddenly felt sorry for him. He wasn't what I'd thought. He said he was bad at conversation. And he was! Still, he tried. That's something I didn't do. Try. If it hadn't been for Joey adopting me into his clan back in preschool, I might not have had any friends at all.

I extended my hand. "My name's Antonia."

His hand hurriedly met mine. "I'm Adolph."

"Adolph. You don't hear that name very often."

"Your first thought was of Hitler, wasn't it?" He forced a laugh. "Well, I spell mine differently than his. I come from a family of three boys. My older brother's named Rudolph, I'm Adolph, and then there's Randolph. Mom called my dad Get-olph."

"For obvious reasons, I'm sure." Again, he laughed, this time more naturally. I just had to add that last statement to put him at ease because he had told this little joke of a story with absolutely no confidence, as though he knew it was a bad idea from the get-go.

"So you said your name was what? I'm sorry. I didn't catch it the first time. I was more concerned about getting through the handshake and my own introduction."

This time I laughed. I liked when people surprised me and weren't at all what they seemed. Anyone looking at him would never have guessed he was anything more than a self-assured twenty-something who handled women with experienced finesse, not some awkward guy who fumbled around trying to find the perfect words for introducing himself.

"Antonia," I repeated.

"Antonia. That's very pretty. But..."

"But what?"

"You just don't look..."

Here we go. "What, ethnic?"

"Just out of curiosity, how'd you get your name?"

"The same way you got yours," I said, with more attitude than was necessary. "What should they have called me, Jane?"

"I don't know." He looked at me skeptically. "Is this a trick question?"

"No. Just go ahead and give me a name that you think really suits me."

"Okay...Elizabeth...Victoria...Diana," he said after only a few seconds of thought.

"Hmm. Not much different than Jane," I said.

"Actually, I was just throwing out the names of British royalty."

"British," I repeated.

"You're right, bad idea. The members of British royalty haven't always been known for their beauty, so maybe they weren't the best choices after all. With your pretty eyes, nice cheekbones, perfect teeth...well, you're more like what royalty should look like."

I rolled my eyes. He didn't even seem to notice as he carried on.

"Confident people tend to look more dignified as well, so maybe that's it. I probably could've left out the name Diana...."

With all its sincerity or insincerity, it was a different answer than I was used to. I liked it, but I had to make it stop now. "All right, Adolph, you can quit with the compliments."

"What did you expect to hear?"

"I expected you to say you chose those names because I look white."

"You're not white?"

"Sorry."

"Why do you apologize for something like that?"

"It wasn't a real apology, Adolph. It was sarcasm."

"Why are you so defensive about who you are?"

"I'm not defensive."

"Then why did you wait, even try trapping me into saying you looked white?"

"I didn't! You know, you're right. You are bad at this." I started to walk off, feeling stupid, immature, and embarrassed.

Adolph ran up ahead of me and stood in my way. "Por favor, Antonia, quédese." He brushed his hand across my arm. It brought chills to the surface, although, they could have come from my surprise at hearing him speak Spanish. "I don't want you to leave on my account. It just seems like no matter how many times I start over with you, I can't seem to get it right." He sighed deeply. "Look, you stay. I'll leave."

I was in the wrong. I knew I had a flare for the dramatic. But I didn't know this guy. I didn't owe him an apology or an explanation. Did I?

"Don't leave, Adolph. I was through writing. I was going to be heading out, anyway, just before you showed up."

"You have somewhere else you need to be?"

Sadly, I actually didn't. But I didn't know what staying would imply. He didn't know me. But then where was I planning to go? What were my options back at camp? Volleyball? Dolores? Eating alone? Bothering the guys at the river? Sleeping? No, not sleeping. I hadn't come all this way to sleep. *Think quick, think quick.*

"Because I don't want to keep you if you have somewhere else to be," Adolph added. His sun-bleached hair glistened in the light. He gleamed like a flint of gold in the sun, smelled like a bar of soap. He was nice enough, too.

I emitted a long, defeated sigh and plopped back down on the sand. "No, I guess I don't have anywhere else I need to be."

"Good. Then we'll keep each other company." He sat

next to me, so close a passerby wouldn't have guessed we were complete strangers.

"Who are you here with?" I asked.

"I'm here by myself. Hitchhiking across the country, stopping at all the interesting places I hear about."

At the mention of the word *hitchhiking*, I immediately thought of the guy from earlier. Adolph looked nothing like the last one. Come to think of it, he looked and smelled a little too clean to be a hitchhiker. The world's biggest loather of stereotypes was about to stereotype. But I couldn't help myself.

"I'm sorry, but I've never seen or smelled such a clean hitchhiker."

"So you've been around a few, eh?"

I didn't gratify the question with an answer. Instead, I quickly asked something else. "Why do you do it? Isn't it dangerous?"

"What, staying clean?"

I nudged him with my elbow. "Hitchhiking, Silly. Why not just drive across the country?"

"I don't need to hitchhike. I do it because it's fun. You get to meet more people, see more places, and have more interesting experiences this way. The danger part just adds to it. It's the thrill of living on the edge. You should try it sometime."

"Not that I'm a big traveler, but I prefer having a motor and air conditioning of my own to get me to a destination."

"Well, it's not about the destination, Antonia. Just like pot, it's all about the trip."

"I wouldn't know about that. Anyway, it's nothing I'd ever try. I'm all for new experiences, but it just sounds way too dangerous."

"Pot or hitchhiking?"

"Both! But hitchhiking..."

"Oh. Well, you have to protect yourself. And don't tell me you've never tried pot."

"I haven't."

"Why not?"

"Well, not that it's any of your business, but burning brain cells and acting like a complete idiot are just things that don't interest me."

Adolph gave a loud sarcastic laugh. "Antonia, you are young. You'll try it eventually."

I didn't bother trying to respond cleverly. I just hoped my silence would suggest we move on. But no such luck.

"You wanna know what I think? I think you want to try it; you've just never been given the opportunity. But that would be an embarrassing thing to admit so it's easier to come across as judgmental."

Enough was enough. "Okay, number one, I've had plenty of opportunities. And number two, just how old do you think I am?"

"Oh, no. Not this game again."

"Come on. Give me a number. I promise not to be defensive, no matter what you say."

"No matter what?" he asked skeptically.

"Well, unless you say something like forty-five...or eleven."

Adolph grinned mischievously and, in even less time than before, he said, "You're eighteen, judging by your levels of both maturity and immaturity. And just so there are no more questions, let me guess about the rest. You are Hispanic, judging by your defensiveness earlier and lack of response when I spoke Spanish to you. You're spoiled, judging by your head-to-toe Gap wear, fancy class ring, diamond studs and manicure," he said, lifting my hand to get a closer look at my nails.

I pulled away quickly. "Immaturity? And for your information, I don't normally have my nails manicured, but I'm graduating and my mom thought it would look nice. Granted, I should've waited 'til after this camping trip." I didn't say what I really wanted to say, which was, *Go to hell! And how dare you! And who do you think you are?* But he was right. About everything.

"Wait a second, I'm not done," he continued. "You have a good Mom, albeit overbearing, and that's why you have a strong sense of morals instead of a wild streak, like most young, repressed teenage Catholics. That's also why you haven't smoked pot. Although she's done a really good job of spoiling you, I suppose you could've bought all this stuff yourself, but I kinda doubt it. She wouldn't let you work, would she?"

I was wrong. This guy was way creepier than the first hitchhiker. "How...?" I started.

Leaning back on his elbows, Adolph stared at his own feet digging in and out of the sand. "How did I know so much about you?" He laughed. "Let's just say I was always better in psychology than communications."

He stopped the digging and looked up at me. "So what happened to your dad?"

"How do you know something happened to my dad?"

"Your response just now. I'm going to guess he isn't in the picture anymore. A divorce?"

I didn't talk about that subject very often. When I did, it was mostly with Joey. But there was something about Adolph that opened me up. His atmosphere was so casual and honest. And I was feeling lonely. He'd caught me at a weak moment. I needed to talk.

"No, not a divorce. But I did lose my dad a long time ago."

"I'm sorry. Is this an uncomfortable subject?" he asked, now sitting so close we were touching shoulders.

"No. Well, yes. Usually. But it's okay."

"So you want to talk about it?"

"That all depends..." I tried to get a feel for safety in his eyes, but I didn't get anything solid. And yet I kept going. "Do you feel like listening?"

"I'm all ears. Talk about anything you want."

I didn't know what to make of this guy whose peculiarity made the hairs on my arms erect.

"When did your dad die?" he asked me.

I felt uncomfortably close to Adolph, but I didn't move. "About fifteen years ago. Mom said our house burned down. My dad didn't make it."

"Man, that's harsh. The rest of you were all right, though?"

"Yes. I don't remember any of it. We lived in California at the time."

"Really, what part?" he asked.

"Outside of San Diego."

"Hmm," he said in a way that I couldn't read into.

"Anyway, when we lost everything, she said she couldn't bear living there. So we moved to Santa Ana."

"Why Santa Ana?"

"She said she just randomly chose it."

"That's kinda weird. So what started the fire?" His pace was unusually quick. He was moving through my history like Cliff Notes does *The Grapes of Wrath*. Like he was trying to hurry up and get to the punch line or climax of my story.

"We don't know for sure, but Mom said the firemen thought it was electrical."

"That's pretty horrible."

"Yeah..." I was feeling the urge to hold my breath.

"You guys lost everything, then?" he continued impassively.

I nodded my head.

"So were you there when the fire started?"

"I don't know."

"You don't know?"

"Like I said, I don't remember anything. And my mom doesn't like to talk about it. It's still an emotional topic for her, even after all these years."

Adolph's face was transparently skeptical and I started to feel defensive.

"What does that look mean? What are you insinuating?"

"Hey, you're reading way too much into this. I have no

idea what happened, and I couldn't even begin to guess what your mother feels."

"Well, you were pretty good about guessing everything else concerning my life."

I suddenly wondered what I was doing talking about my deepest feelings to a total stranger. I was airing out my family's missing laundry, and for what? I wasn't covering new territory. This wasn't making me feel any better, either. I wasn't used to feeling defensive about my mother, having her integrity questioned, or mine for that matter. It was my fault for opening up. But I was just so used to Joey's sympathy, Javen's indifference, and Sonny's humor about the situation. They never added to my suspicions, never made my mom out to be a conniver. They just listened nonjudgmentally, Joey especially. *God, why isn't it his shoulder pressed up against mine?*

"So do you have family over there that you keep up with?"

I didn't answer. I was done. That's when he finally got a clue.

"Maybe talking about this wasn't such a good idea after all. What do you say we change the subject?"

"I'd say that's probably a good idea." I put some distance between our shoulders. He just moved closer.

"So how did you hear about the San Francisco Springs, anyway?" I asked, moving farther away as though to get a better look at him as he spoke.

"I don't remember, really. I talk to lots of people. Someone somewhere along the line must've told me about it," he said. And then something occurred to him. "You never told me who you were here with."

"I'm here with friends," I said, trying to hide my sadness. This guy had an uncanny ability to bring every one of my sensations out into the open, except the sensation of discomfort, which he purposefully ignored.

"And where are they?"

"All over. My closest friends are on the river right now, inner-tubing."

"Why aren't you with them?"

"Because...well, it's sort of an all-guy kind of a thing. And since all my close friends happen to be guys, and... well, obviously I'm not. No offense, but that's why I'm sitting here with you."

"None taken. It's just lucky for me you aren't a guy. But I think if I were your close friend, I'd be making an exception to the rule and making sure you came along. That or I wouldn't be at the river."

"Well, there's not exactly a rule that says I can't be there. I just thought I'd let them have time together since we're graduating."

"All the more reason for you to be included."

I smiled sadly, feeling alone all of a sudden. They cared about me, I knew they did...I was pretty sure they did... Joey did. *Why the hell am I letting this stranger be so close to me?*

"You know what, Adolph? I should probably be going. I'm getting hungry." I began to stand up again, but he gently pulled me back.

"Wait. Come eat with me," he said, holding onto my hand. "I have sandwiches in my backpack. Come on, I'll show you. I even have a blanket we can sit on and cups to drink from."

Enough with all the touching! I stood up. "That's okay, really. I think I'll catch up with my friends now."

Just then I heard, "Antonia!"

Joey! He sent a gush of warm relief flowing through my veins.

I waved. "Over here!"

"Hey! What happened to you?" he asked as he approached us. "I thought you were going to be with Dolores? I was looking for you."

"I changed my mind."

Joey looked at Adolph. Adolph looked at Joey. To alleviate the awkward silence that followed, I introduced the two.

Adolph extended his hand first. "So this is Joey."
Joey looked bewildered. So did I. I hadn't mentioned
Joey's name before. He sounded as though I'd already told
him all about Joey.

Joey accepted his handshake. "Nice meeting you...
Adolph, was it?"

"Yup." Adolph abruptly turned his attention back to
me. "So, are we getting something to eat?"

My expression must have said, *You've got to be kidding
me! Why would I do that? Especially now, with Joey here.
Joey, for crying out loud!* I hoped that's what it said, since
he was so good at reading me.

But I remained polite. "No thank you. I'm leaving with
Joey now. Thank you for your company. It was really fun
talking to you. And, hey, good luck on your journey across
the country."

Once again, Adolph grabbed my hand. "Please? Please
join me. I'm all by myself, remember?"

Before I could reject him again, Joey responded. "She's
coming with me now, Adolph." He grabbed my other hand
and started pulling until Adolph reluctantly let go.

I could hear him laughing as we hurried away. We were
no more than ten yards off when he shouted, "Does your
inner-tubing boyfriend there know about Matthew?"

I couldn't believe what I was hearing! My cheeks were
instantly aflame. Who the hell was this guy I had just sat
down with and poured my life story out to? He continued to
laugh, but I refused to turn around and look.

"What's that idiot rambling on about? And what were
you doing with a strange guy like that, anyway?"

"He must have been reading over my shoulder a lot
longer than he admitted to. I always address my journal to
my dad. He must have seen the name Matthew." *And Joey.*

"Idiot is right," I mumbled, only I wasn't referring to
Adolph. I was referring to myself.

"He called me your boyfriend. Is that what you told
him?"

"Of course not!" Long pause. Too long. I had to fill the silence. "Like you said, he was just an idiot. He made lots of assumptions based on a whole lot of nothing."

Joey was still holding my hand. We could have been together. We could have been a couple. Only he was angry. It was more like the way a father would hold his child's hand after she'd wandered off in a busy mall.

"You should've just stayed at camp like you said you were."

I wanted to pour my heart out to him right then and there. But I couldn't. "Next time I'll take someone with me," I said like an obedient child.

It wasn't the time. Not yet. It didn't feel quite right. Not with him scolding me for my stupidity.

"Next time you'll take *me* with you," he said before trailing off into an apology. "I'm sorry for ditching you, Antonia. That wasn't a very cool thing to do."

"I didn't need a babysitter, Joe."

"That's true. But I'm pretty sure you could've used your best friend."

"That's true. Lucky for me he showed up just in time."

Joey squeezed my hand.

"Speaking of my best friend, he wasn't at the river very long. What happened?"

"Well, actually, I wanted to talk to you about something."

Chapter 2
Joey's Story

There once was a man who took his stepchildren fishing at a dam near Casas Grandes. He never liked the two boys much, so they were both very surprised at the invitation and yet a little frightened. They had never been to a lake before."

Papá lays his fishing rod down and stands up. Picking up a rock, he throws it angrily across the river.

"What happened, Papá?" I ask.

"The stepfather decided they needed to learn how to swim. So he pushed them both off the boat and made them swim to shore."

"Did they learn?'

"Only one of them learned."

My dad sits back down and turns his back to me.

"The one that didn't learn was going to grow up to be a farmer. He had plans to move to America and grow food for a living. Work for himself, tu sabes? But that never got to happen."

"Why not?" I asked.

"Because he drowned that day, mi'jito. His name was Carlos. He was your age."

The birds, the wind, the river, they all come to my dad's rescue and permeate the quiet between us. It was one of the few times in my life when I had no words to fill the silence with.

"I have no education. No money. But I have my memory," he says. "It's important to remember things, mi'jo. To remember where you came from, the good things, but just as importantly, the bad things. It's the memories that taste bitter in your mouth that push you forward. Valora tus memorias y aprende de ellas."

Sonny remembers the year he turned eight as the year he thought he saw his grandmother's ghost. I remember it as the year my father became an official United States citizen, the last time I went to the Gila, and the first time I understood what Papá meant about the importance of remembering.

Papá had taken Mamá, my little sister Ramona and me to the Gila National Forest to celebrate, visit the cliff dwellings, and fish. It was in the late spring, after an unusually wet winter. Snowfall reached record levels that year. And then, suddenly, the temperatures warmed up fast causing the snowmelt to flood this little river's banks, taking soil and anything else that tried slowing it down right along with it. The sediment caused an increase in the number of meanders in the river valley, all resembling hot chocolate more so than water.

We picked a faster-flowing one with a deep pool in it. Perfect for fishing, Papá had said. It didn't matter to me. That river could've been bone dry and I wouldn't have cared. It was nice just to be with him, to see him so happy and relaxed and proud, not drenched in sweat, smelling like tractor oil or chile and onions, whatever the latest crop was he had helped harvest. That was the first time Papá had ever taken us fishing and, for one reason or another, it turned out to be the last.

Ramona was asleep when we found a place to park. From the start, my parents must have known it wasn't a serious fishing trip. They brought plenty of other food just in case. No waiting around for rainbow trout that day, and thankfully so. We never did catch anything.

Papá still had lots of ambition in his eyes, even as Mamá unpacked the hamburger and hot dogs and started a fire. He took off his jacket and wrapped it around

Ramona, who slept nice and cozy in the cab of our old Chevy pickup patched in Bondo, painted primer gray, and almost always caked in mud. He kissed Mamá's forehead and thanked her before grabbing our borrowed fishing sticks with one hand, a small tackle-box with the other. Then he motioned with his head for me to follow. We walked to a place where there was a fallen tree. He pointed at it with the tackle box hand.

"This is the place, mi'jo. No chairs. We don't want to tire."

I had never fished before, and so I watched him carefully as he took out a little jar from the green box filled with hooks, sinkers, floats, and plastic worms. Everything looked new and unused, including the green box and the hot-pink marshmallowy cream in his jar. After taking out a dab and rolling it into a ball, he handed it to me to stick on the hook at the end of my line. I wanted to eat it myself; it looked like bubble gum. But when I put it up to my nose I quickly realized it was definitely not something sweet. It smelled more like garlic.

I walked to the edge of the river and dipped my line into the water.

"Like this." He grabbed my rod and walked a few paces back toward the log. Still standing, he showed me how to properly cast my line. I remember how everything sounded so crisp and separate. The zip of my fishing line as it flew through the air. The churning of the river, the soft wind blowing through the valley. The jostling of rocks beneath Papá's feet like he was standing on ice cubes as he shifted his weight from one foot to the other. The gentle plop of the small, silver sinkers landing on water. And then the clicking of the reel as he wound it back in.

He handed it back to me. "Now you try."

It took some practice, but I finally got the hang of it.

I could tell Papá was proud of me as he cast his own line into the water and made himself comfortable on the log. He wore his old John Deere cap, a faded brown and blue flannel shirt, and Levi's so worn and stained nobody would have known they were fresh from the dryer. Nobody would have known he was one of the wisest men in all of New Mexico, either.

"All that soil tan precioso, running down the river like it has somewhere important it needs to go to," he said as we fished.

For all I cared, the river could have every last bit of that stupid soil. It was what my dad slaved over every day. It was what his shoes smeared into our beat-up carpet, and what his fingernails permanently harbored. It's what kept him away all the time. *Let the water take it away*, I thought.

"Too much water. It's like anything else, you don't want too much of a good thing, not all at one time. ¿Qué no?"

I didn't answer him. I was focused on the end of my line, the float moving up and down, up and down ever-so-lightly in conjunction with the waves of the muddy river.

"Did you know that those Indians who lived up in the cliff dwellings, los Mogollónes, they were farmers? They grew things like corn and beans and squash.

"Tell me, mi'jito, what do you want to be when you grow up?"

Papá dreamed of being a farmer, working for himself, owning his own piece of America, making his brother's dreams come true. He would spend a good deal of time convincing me to join in that dream.

"A truck driver," I answered with absolute certainty.

"A truck driver! You want to drive a truck every day? Never get to see your family? Never get to eat Mami's albóndigas?"

"I'll just have her pack me some for the road."

"A Thermos is okay for chicken noodles, but meatball soup, mi'jito? And besides that, you'd probably see tu Mamá once a month, si tienes suerte. Truck drivers spend all their time driving trucks."

Maybe truck driving wasn't what I wanted to be after

all. I thought a little while longer. "Maybe I'll just be a baseball player," I said.

"Have you thought about farming?"

At eight? Of course I hadn't. I didn't even know the difference between a farmer and a farmhand. So as far as I was concerned, Papá was a farmer, a slave to the land, doing hard, sweaty labor for little pay. It was shameful. So why would I want to grow up and be a slave? He wasn't cool and interesting like Sonny's dad. Sonny's dad was a football coach. Javen's dad owned his own grocery store, the same store Papá stocked with produce. Antonia didn't have a dad, but even her mom had a decent job. She was a high school teacher back then.

"Farming just isn't cool, Papá," I said, as gently as I could.

"¿No es qué?"

"It's not cool. I wanna do something important when I grow up."

My dad laughed loudly. "And you think baseball is cool and important, hombre?

"Let me tell you something, José. If every baseball player and every truck driver quit tomorrow, life would go on. Life would be a little tougher, maybe a little less fun, but it would go on. Pero if every farmer quit tomorrow, this world would be in a lot of trouble."

"But we never have enough money."

"Money isn't everything. We have important things, qué no? We have food, a home, amor. That's a lot for someone who isn't even a true farmer yet, no?

"But you just wait, Someday soon we will own a piece of this country. Not because it will give us mas dinero or pride, but because we can. When you go from somewhere that you can't to somewhere that you can, you sure as hell better, no?"

It was a lot for an eight-year-old to take in. But after he told me about his brother, somehow I understood.

"When do you think you will be your own farmer?" I asked.

"Someday, mi'jito. We gotta start from the bottom and work our way up, so that when the time comes, there isn't anything we don't know or can't do. It's a big dream, but we can do it together. ¿Entiendes, Méndez?"

"Si, Papá."

"¿Me vas ayudar? No lo puedo hacer solo. I need your smarts."

"Sure, Papá, I'll help you."

Ten years later, he still wasn't a farmer. He was saving his pennies and waiting on me. My education. My smarts. Everything was riding on me. I did my part by making the grades. But without a college degree Papá said it would all be for nothing. So we attended workshops together on how to find and apply for scholarships. We collected cans for cash. Mami even raised money by selling enchilada dinner plates every Sunday since the day I started junior high school. It was all about my grades. That's why Papá wouldn't let me work during the school year. But as an incentive for good grades, I was given an allowance. It was just enough to get me a used truck and pay for gas. Summers were my only money-making opportunities, and so I did hard labor because it paid well. I sacked onions down at Simmons' Farms, mowed lawns around town, even baled hay for Antonia's mother, Ms. Pacheco.

Texas A & M. That's where Papá thought I could get the best education that money could buy in the field of agriculture. The day I was accepted was the happiest day of his life. I still hadn't told him I would be class valedictorian. That surprise would come on graduation day when I would walk up to the podium and give my speech.

Tan preciosa, la güera. That's what my dad would say every time Antonia's name came up or she walked out of a room. ¿Por qué no estás con ella?

"Because we're just friends. She doesn't think of me like that, Papá."

Or does she?

I looked down at our fingers still mingling with one

another like stringy cheese on calabacitas. There were a million thoughts running through my head: graduation, my speech, Antonia, my Papá. Strangely, though, food was right at the top.

"Have you eaten something?" she asked me as we made our way back to the campsite.

"Not yet. But I'm not hungry," I lied, hoping she couldn't hear the noises, like a jabalí, coming from my stomach. How do I break away? It was too early. And then I saw something.

"Look!" I let loose and pointed.

"What is it?"

"There, under that tree." I gently turned her head in the right direction. "See that little bird there, the one that's walking instead of hopping like most birds? See it? It has a black stripe under its eye and a white one above."

She nodded.

"That's a horned lark. You don't normally see those up in the mountains. They're usually in open areas."

I got very quiet so she could hear the soft "ti-ti" sounds it was making. We had to strain to hear over the river and the music, the whooping and the hollering. Even the wind competed for our attention. But the little lark didn't seem to care that his song was drowning in a sea of aggressive noises.

We continued walking back to the campsite without touching. I pointed out other birds I recognized — the acorn woodpecker, the tree swallow, the western tanager.

"How do you know so much, Joey?" she asked, even if she already knew the answer.

I shrugged like I always do.

She shook her head. A part of me hated to talk like I knew everything. I knew what Javen and Sonny thought about it, so I kept deep conversation to a minimum when they were around. But Antonia was different. "Tell me about the Mogollón...the cliff dwellers...show me Venus and Jupiter," she'd say.

Some guys collected baseball cards or arrowheads; shot glasses and phone numbers. I collected information. It wasn't tangible, but it was a lot more retrievable at a moment's notice than fishing trophies, and a heck of a lot more useful than autographed t-shirts. Cheaper, too. I knew it fascinated her to no end when I did something like I was doing now — describing the subtle differences between the copper's and sharp-shinned hawks. That was reason enough to continue my bad habit of telling her every useless story, fact, or morsel of information I'd ever learned.

So I was more than just a little surprised that she wasn't asking me the obvious question. Once I quit talking, she was bound to ask me what my question was. Not that I gave her much opportunity, but she didn't ask. She was deep in her own thoughts, a galaxy away from me.

When we made it back to camp. Antonia grabbed us some cans of soda; I fixed two plates of food for us, chips and cheeseburgers. And then we walked, and walked, and walked. We looked for a picnic table, any decent place to sit and eat where the flies and seniors hadn't gotten thick yet. We finally settled on two nice-sized rocks fairly close to one another. She stared at her burger like it was too overwhelming to eat. When she started to tear off tiny pieces of her bun and feed them to a nearby chipmunk, I finally asked, "Are you okay?"

"Yeah," she said without looking at me.

I felt strange eating when she wasn't, so I started feeding the chipmunk, too.

"You should eat that," she said.

"You should, too," I replied. Still, she kept on tossing bread crumbs to the lucky little rodent at her feet.

I took the plate from her. "All right, Antonia." I said her name the right way, not the lazy way we always did. It got her attention. "What's up with you?"

"I'm sorry, Joe. I really don't know what my problem is.... Maybe you should just go catch up with Sonny and Jav."

"No, don't give me that. I'm not going anywhere, especially when something is bugging you...is it me? Is it
that—"

"No, it isn't you," she cut in. "It's just...you know, I've
been looking forward to this day for a year...so why isn't it
living up to all my expectations?"

"Did you want to go down to the river? We can do anything you want to."

"It's not that."

"Was it that guy Adolph?"

"He probably has something to do with it, but it's more
than that."

I was getting frustrated. I was usually better at this,
about figuring out what was bothering her. But I was just
as distracted as she was. Then she really surprised me.

"What do you think was the deal with that old
hitchhiker?"

I suppose he was strange, and maybe I should have
been more concerned. But I knew there had to be an explanation for it; I just hadn't tried to figure it out yet. "Is that
what's bothering you?"

"Every time I try thinking of other things, my mind
wanders back to him. Adolph was a hitchhiker, too. It's all
just weird, don't you think?" She came over to my rock and
scooted me over.

If this was the true problem, I thought I could easily
put her mind at ease. Then she would be brought back to
the moment, and there wouldn't be anything stopping her
from wondering what I wanted to ask her earlier. ¡Ay! But
it had to be done. I couldn't let her go on being preoccupied
and upset.

I looked down at my watch, then into her gray eyes.
"You got a minute to hear me out?"

She laughed. "I'll make time for you."

"All right. A long time ago there was this ghostly figure
who rode on the back of a black stallion in southwest
Texas. He was dressed like a Mexican vaquero, wearing

rawhide leggings, a buckskin jacket, an old shawl. And above the shoulders where a head should've been there was nothing but a wide sombrero. This thing could appear at any time of day, roaming across the open range. And it was always alone.

"No one doubted its existence because too many people saw it. People would even shoot at it, but the bullets seemed to just go straight through it.

"One day some of the riders decided to put an end to the mystery and hunt down this phantom rider. A bunch of 'em got together and waited for it at a watering hole. When the mustang finally appeared, they opened fire, and the horse fell dead to the ground. The mystery would finally be solved.

"They went over to the horse and found a dried-up corpse full of bullets. Under the sombrero was his skull. They eventually found out who the dead man was. He was a guy named Vidal, a horse thief. He had been killed by a veteran of the Mexican War and, as a warning to other rustlers, left to ride out wild on the range, his decapitated body tied to the stallion.

"Can you imagine how many people were screwed up from seeing that? But in the end, there was an explanation for all of it.

"I guess what I'm trying to say is that you don't need to dwell on the unknowns. Just trust that there's an explanation and let it go."

She smiled and I knew she was going to be okay. "You're right. I'm officially letting it go. It's stupid of me to waste another second thinking about it."

"Good," I said.

"Good," she repeated.

"So..." she began. "What did you want to ask me earlier?"

I knew it.

Truth be told, I always filled the air with my voice because I didn't want my heart to start speaking for me, not until I was ready. I still wasn't ready. The truth is that I got more pleasure from standing next to Antonia in silence than from the bullshitting I did with my other friends. She was going to one college and I would be going to another. A part of me saw no point in putting myself out there, laying my feelings on the line. It wouldn't be fair to either of us. But I was so tired of lying and hiding under the cloak of our friendship. My time was up.

"You remember those expensive sunglasses you bought for Sonny at Christmas?"

"What about them?" she asked.

"He can't find 'em. So I offered to help look for them, and..."

"You want me to help?"

"Do you mind?"

"I'll do it for you," she said with a wink.

***

"Remind me again why we're out here?" I asked hours later.

"We're looking for Sonny's sunglasses."

"No, what I meant was, remind me again why we're out here and Sonny isn't."

"Well, because now he's too drunk, because we're about the only sober people left, because it's getting dark, because they were expensive, and because we expect him to pay back our kindness very nicely. Am I leaving anything out?"

Yes, it gives us another reason to be alone, I wanted to add but kept silent.

It was getting past the point of ridiculous. I had to say something. I'd let too many perfect opportunities pass and whiled away too many hours skidding rocks across the river or collecting firewood, all the while pretending to search for Sonny's sunglasses.

The sun was about to set. I had no idea where the day had gone.

I watched Antonia's studious expression as she searched the area surrounding her. She was such a good friend to me, to all of us, for that matter. She would do anything for us. I was having doubts. Maybe wanting more was wrong. Maybe I should have been satisfied with the friendship we had.

Then she looked up at me with those gray eyes of hers. And at that moment, all doubt was erased. It was right. We were right. She had to see it now. It was time.

"Joey!" she shouted.

"What!" I burst out.

"I found them! Right here in these rocks. Does Sonny have the luck of the Irish or what? Isn't he part Irish?"

I couldn't believe it. What were the odds of finding anything as small as a pair of sunglasses in a three-million-acre forest?

"Thank you for helping me look for them, Joe."

"I thought *you* were the one helping *me*," I replied.

But Antonia wasn't listening. She was trying not to sneeze as white fibers from the cottonwoods floated in the breeze and down the river.

We'd searched miles along the river's banks, and now goosebumps were emerging all over our bodies as the sun disappeared behind the canyon walls. I was on my feet by this time, putting my shoes back on and walking back to camp, feeling cursed and hopeless. Things weren't turning out as I had planned and anger was creeping in.

"Sonny's probably forgotten all about those stupid sunglasses by now, with all the drinking he's done," I said bitterly.

I was a few steps ahead of Antonia, but I could still hear her as she stopped walking and stood silent. I turned around to face her. She was staring at me. "You sound upset about that. I mean, didn't you know he was going to be drinking today?"

"Yeah, I knew." What I didn't know was how to explain away my tone. "I just don't know why we wasted so much time."

"I thought we were having fun together. I'm sorry you feel like you've been wasting time," she finally said after what seemed like an excessively drawn-out silence.

I walked over to Antonia and wrapped an arm around her, squeezed her tight and gave her a rub for warmth, suddenly feeling thankful for Sonny's drunkenness and for being stupid enough to wear his high-dollar sunglasses while inner-tubing.

"I didn't make myself clear," I said as we started walking again. "Spending the day with you wasn't a waste of time. Spending our time looking for something as ridiculous as sunglasses was. We should have been...."

Antonia smiled. And that was my cue. It was now or never.

"Listen, I know I've done my fair share of drinking in the past, but that shot of whiskey I took this morning with Javen and Sonny was the only drink I had today."

"Yeah, I noticed that," she said. "And I'm glad. But I'd be lying if I said I wasn't surprised. I thought that's what you came here to do."

This time I stopped walking. "That's not why I came here today, Antonia." I paused, looked into her eyes and found the reassurance that I needed to continue. "I wanted to stay sober today so I could be completely aware when I said what I wanted to say. But now that I'm here, and the day is almost over, I'm sort of wishing I had drunk something, anything, because it might have given me the courage I need to —"

"Joey, wait..."

"No, I need to tell you this. I've waited way too long."

"I need to tell you something too," she said.

"Ladies should go first, I know. But if I don't say this right now, I don't know when I'll get enough nerve to do it again."

I wiped my sweaty hands on my jeans, still shivering as I tried to remember the words I wanted to say.

"First, let's find a place to sit," I said, searching the

area surrounding us. But there wasn't a single, solitary place suitable for a young lady to sit. No big rocks, no fallen logs. Meanwhile, Antonia was starting to worry. "Is this bad? Because I think I can handle it. I don't have to be sitting."

"No, no, no. It's nothing bad. Well, I hope you don't think it's bad. I just thought you'd be more comfortable sitting. I have a lot I need to say."

I took Sonny's sunglasses out of her hands and hung them from my back pocket so that I could take both of her hands in mine. I was surprised to discover they were just as clammy as mine.

"I'm not like you," I said. "I don't have a poetic bone in my body. I can tell you all about poets, but you know better than anyone that poetry just isn't my thing.

"And yet I wanted to write something for you, Antonia…a long time ago, when I realized how I felt. And… well, I thought I'd share it with you today, before it's too late…I could never tell you how I felt before now."

She started to cry and laugh at the same time. I, the eternal optimist, took that as a good sign since she never cried.

"Prepare yourself for something really bad because like I said —"

"Joey!"

"All right. All right." And so I started. "It's called 'The Color of a Star.'" She wiped her tears and giggled at me.

"Softer than pink, warmer than brown. More beautiful than silver and blue. Stronger than black, braver than red. More spirited than yellow's spry hue." I put our clasped hands up to my chest and continued. "You are purer than white…"

I stopped. We both grew very quiet. Someone had screamed. It was followed by the sound of muffled cries.

What timing. We looked at each other, for one or the other to say, *Let's just ignore it.* But we both knew that we couldn't.

"I'll go see what's going on. You wait here for me?"

"No way. We're going together." She grabbed my hand. "But first...was that the end, or was there more?"

"There was more."

"Then as soon as we find out what that noise was, we're going somewhere quiet and warm — the Suvee — so I can hear the rest."

I gave her hand a tight squeeze as we walked in the direction of the mysterious yelling.

Chapter 3
Javen's Story

Eddie played a damn good guitar. He knew nothing but Spanish songs, but that was cool with me. I gave credit where credit was due. Now, whether it was sunrises or sandwiches he was singing about, I couldn't tell. I mostly knew mari words — mariscos, mariachis, mariposas, marijuana. That last one I knew all too well. Anyway, none of those words were in his song. Still, it was pretty nice. Bush, the band, was ruining the moment, blaring in the background about the little things that kill. But it wasn't as bad as Tommy pretending he knew the words to Eddie's song as he tried singing along in his faux-Mexican accent.

Poor Tom was a wannabe-Mexican. And Eddie was his hero. Friggin' Eddie just played the part, sitting back and strumming, letting his girlfriend braid his hair. His long, straight, black hair. You'd a thought the guy was Indian, if it wasn't for him constantly reminding everyone of how "Chicano" he was. Him and Joey both. They were prouder than peacocks of their genetic makeup, as though they had a choice in the matter. I hated that shit.

Race, ethnicity, breed, clan, tribe — what the hell was the point of categorizing? Antonia looked white but wasn't. Tommy was white but wished he wasn't. Sonny was obviously black, but raised by everything else. Eddie looked Indian, and I...well, who gave a shit, anyway? I didn't.

I didn't care about my race so much as what was taking Joey so long. From where I sat, I could see him standing a good distance from camp with Antonia. *Looking for Sonny's sunglasses.* Talk about your lame excuses.

I took a long swig from my bottle and decided I'd give them a few more minutes before I made Joey regret ever leaving with her in the first place.

I couldn't believe it was Joey who was about to betray me, of all people. There were two things I counted on to get me through each day — my feet and my friends. I trusted my feet to come to my rescue when all else failed. I trusted my friends for the very same reason. I still couldn't get over it. Joey!

It wasn't as if he didn't know about Antonia and me. In fact, he was the one who'd played cupid. I ended up dating her on and off for three months the year before. It was the best three months of my life.

As far back as I can remember Antonia was in the picture. I should actually thank Ms. Pacheco for it; Antonia and I might not've been so close if Ms. Pacheco hadn't felt so sorry for me. She's the one who was always inviting me over, not Antonia. Of course, Mom didn't object.

Ms. P would do things like enroll the both of us in summer swimming lessons and then stay and watch us the whole time. I couldn't believe how lucky Antonia was, for having someone so interested, following her every move. At the time, I'd've killed for that kind of attention. But I guess the grass is always greener on the other side. She thought I was lucky to not have my mother's shadow always hovering overhead.

Anyway, I thought of Antonia as a sister for a long, long time. But neither of us stayed ten forever. She wasn't voluptuous, not in the least. But she was beautiful. There's something to be said about healthy hair, perfect teeth, clear skin and eyes that can knock a man down to his knees. I, of course, became one of those guys that took notice. But it was more than just her looks — it was her confidence, her wit, her complete presence when I kissed her...the way she could make a roomful of people disappear by giving me all of her attention as if no one else existed.

But me being who I am, I pushed things too far. She freaked out, of course...started talking about how different we were and shit. I tried to tell her how it was in my blood; I would've told her everything if she'd've given me a chance. But she didn't. From then on, we were "just friends."

Anyway, she'd already broken the friendship code with me. She couldn't do it with another one of us. She wouldn't. Not unless Joey put on the pressure. Then she might.

I thought Joey knew that you don't hit on your friend's ex; I don't care how small the town is or how few fish there are in the water. As far as I was concerned, he'd already had his chance and blown it. He had kindergarten through the start of eleventh grade to get it right. It was too late now. It wasn't my fault he chose to be a chicken-shit.

Besides, it was common knowledge that I still wasn't over her. It might not've been something I yelled from the treetops...but I kept her in my life.

There was still hope. If she'd hated me, I'd say it was over. But we were still friends. She even trusted me with her Suvee, me — pot-smoking, fly-by-the-seat-of-his-pants, don't-give-a-shit, crazy-motherfuckin' me. Now with Joey using this "let's-go-find-Sonny's-sunglasses-for-him-so-we-can-be-all-alone-when-it-gets-dark" crap with her, my chances of pulling things back together were getting slimmer and slimmer with every minute that passed.

I took one last drink before throwing the empty bottle into the fire. I wanted to scream my head off. I'd've kicked the shit out of someone if they touched me at that moment.

I searched the sky for some peace. It was turning that bluish-gray color right before dark, the color of Antonia's eyes. I reached for my wallet, opened it and pulled out a thick letter that Antonia had written to me while vacationing in eastern Oklahoma during Spring Break last year. I really didn't need to read it all; I had the whole three pages memorized.

It was really the last five words I cared about: Con todo mi amor, Antonia.

It was the first and last letter she'd ever write me.

We make better friends, anyway, Jav. Those were her exact words when she came back. But she couldn't look me in the eyes as she said them. At the time, I thought it was my dope-smoking that pushed her over the edge. I wasn't so sure anymore.

"Con todo mi amor." I didn't know a lot of Spanish, but I knew what those words meant. *With all my love.* How could she say that to me if she didn't mean it? And if she meant it, how could those feelings just die overnight? Because I knew what it felt like to love someone. She could break down and tell me she was addicted to kissing goldfish and chewing tobacco and I'd still love her. I just didn't get it.

I guess it didn't matter because at the end of the day, she was with Joey. Fucking 4H-loving, clod-kicking, ass-kissing Joey. What did he have that I didn't besides an FFA jacket and a 4.5 GPA? Maybe I needed to find out.

I looked back up to where they had been standing. But they were gone. Which was probably a good thing because I'd worked myself up enough that I was ready to kill the son of a bitch.

I interrupted Tommy and Eddie's duet. "Where's Sonny?" I asked.

"¿Quién sabe?" Eddie answered.

"Who cares, Dude?" Tommy added.

I stood up and searched all the drunken faces around me. But I couldn't find Sonny's anywhere. I asked anyone who looked sober enough to answer.

"Shelby, where's Sonny?"

"Rob, you seen Sonny?"

"Julie wake up! Where's Santino?"

"I thought I saw him puking over there behind Antonia's truck," she said in a drunken stupor.

"It's an SUV."

"Truck, SUV, whatever." She pointed me in the wrong direction.

I shook my head in disgust. "Dopehead," I mumbled. "Speaking of dopes, where's Dolores? That girl owes me ten bucks."

"She took off with some guy from L.A. she met at the springs."

"Figures," I said as I walked around to the back of the Suvee.

Sonny was right where Julie said he would be, as sick as she said, too.

"What the hell are you doin'?" I asked him as I popped open the back, pulled out a towel and threw it into his face.

"Admiring Tonia's tires. What do you think I'm doing?"

"Get the fuck up already!" I said, kicking him in the ass. "I can't believe you! Couldn't you hold down your alcohol at least 'til the moon came out?"

"Javen, what do you want? And how much money will it take to get you to go away?"

"Get up. We're going to go look for Joe and Antonia."

"What for?"

"Don't worry about it. Let's just go."

Chapter 4
Joey's Story

Camp was a million miles away. I could barely make out the light of the fire, the slinky smoke rising into the air, the distant sound of laughing, yelling, Eddie's guitar.

Antonia and I crept through the woods toward the rustling sound growing louder with every step we took.

"Listen," I whispered as we stopped for a moment. "It sounds like —"

"Don't say it. I know," she whispered back. It was too dark to tell, but I knew she was blushing at the mere thought of me saying the word "sex."

"Maybe it's nothing to worry about," I said, hopefully.

But then there was the muffled yell again.

"Let's just check it out."

We continued moving toward the sound as it grew louder.

Before we could gather our thoughts or prepare ourselves, we came upon the noise, frozen with disbelief at the sight of the two familiar bodies lying on the ground. One of them was Dolores. Her mouth was gagged shut with a t-shirt. Her half-living, half-dead body looked as though it had been yanked through the forest's thorny, stony, murky bottom up to the very spot where she lay now. Only a thin layer of dust covered the bruises and blood across the length of her naked body. Grass and debris were entangled in her hair, her arms tied up above her head to the trunk of a tree with a thick blue nylon rope. Adolph, unaware of our presence, continued to rape her.

I will never forget the look on their faces. Both Dolores' and Antonia's. Dolores was disappearing faster than the sun's light. Her face was empty, separated from her body. Antonia's was overwhelmed with horror, fear and... *what if it had been her?* My thoughts went from Dolores, to Antonia, to the realization that I had to do something.

I shook off my fear, lunging at Adolph and tearing their bodies apart. I watched him lying face down on the ground, yanking up his shorts, all the while feeling as though I were swimming in mud. I couldn't move fast enough, scream loud enough, hit hard enough. I was in a bad dream.

I tried my hardest to shout, "Antonia! Get out of here! Go get Javen!" But I wasn't sure she could hear me. I wasn't even sure the words were coming out. I fought to control Adolph's squirming body, fumbling with his arms and hands, his feet and hair, anything I could grab. Antonia ran to Dolores and ungagged her mouth. She tried covering her body with her torn clothing and tried to undo the knot biting into her wrists.

"Get up, Dolores! You have to help me!" she pleaded. But Dolores was limp and quivering, falling to the ground every time Antonia attempted to lift her.

I started to panic as I realized that Dolores could die, *would* die if she didn't get help. Adolph struggled to get loose; the night was getting darker and it was getting harder to see around me.

"Just leave her there for a second and go get help, Antonia!" I screamed.

"I'm not leaving her and I'm not leaving you!"

"I can handle it! Just go!"

"No, you can't, Joey," Adolph said calmly.

There was silence just before the shot rang out.

I looked at Antonia. She looked at Adolph, then at me.

Before I could see who was shot, I fell to my knees, then down to my back. I felt my face, my chest, then moved my hand down to my stomach where I felt the hole in the cloth. I lifted my shirt and felt blood.

Antonia screamed words I couldn't understand as she let Dolores fall to the ground. She ran to my side and pulled me onto her lap. With her hand, she tried to stop the blood seeping through my shirt more quickly now.

Adolph turned his attention back to Dolores. He stood over her and shot her in the head with the cruel indifference of his Nazi namesake, if that was even his real name. He had managed to dress himself without my even noticing. And, unbelievably, he had managed to get a gun.

"Why are you doing this?" Antonia screamed.

He studied her face, smiling flirtatiously. "That's not what you'd really like to know, now is it, Antonia?" he finally said.

He walked over and knelt down beside her, then moved closer, rubbed his hand down her back and whispered in her ear. "It was you I really wanted."

She pulled me closer. I could hear and feel her heart pounding against my head. I could also tell that she was holding her breath, just the way she used to do when we were kids.

Adolph stood up and walked toward Dolores. He ripped the rope off her wrists, the same rope Antonia seemed to work at for hours. He stuffed it and the wadded-up t-shirt he'd used to gag her into his backpack.

As he gathered up his belongings, I reached up and grabbed Antonia's hand, the hand cradling my head. I gave it a reassuring squeeze. She gasped. I closed my eyes and played dead again.

Adolph turned. "What?"

"Nothing."

He was quiet for a long moment. I wanted so badly to open my eyes to read his intentions. But I had to wait. Soon he was busy at his bag again. I opened my eyes and looked up at Antonia. She was looking at me, too. I smiled and caught one of her tears on my forehead. She smiled back. I knew she was thinking the same thing I was thinking.

Adolph zipped his bag shut and we resumed our parts

in his game. He walked over to Antonia. She shielded my eyes with her hand, holding my head to keep Adolph from knowing I was alive. I squinted through the cracks in her fingers.

"You realize I'm faced with a real dilemma. I can let you live. And you will always remember that good-looking hitchhiker who knew you better than anyone you've ever met. Or I can kill you now. So you can join your not-so-good-looking friends in the afterlife. If I do the latter, I won't ever have to worry about you haunting me later."

Antonia smiled. "I'll haunt you either way, Adolph." She was getting brave. I didn't like it. She wasn't talking to another smartass. This wasn't Javen.

Adolph found it amusing. "Now there's the Antonia I know and love." He let the gun in his hand fall limp. He sat on his haunches, facing her, "You really are too beautiful to kill...just yet."

"What do you want?" she asked, her head high.

"Do I have to say it?"

"Yeah, you have to say it. Nothing's free."

He laughed. "I don't think —"

"Say it!"

Adolph smiled. "Let's not ruin the moment, okay?"

"What do you want, Adolph?"

He rested his hand on her cheek and let it glide down her neck, breast, waist....

I tried to stand, but I was held firm by her arms. My body couldn't accomplish what my heart told me to do. I didn't even have the strength to cry for her.

And then there was a noise. Adolph stood up and turned around. It was Sonny! He was standing behind him, holding Adolph's bag. I didn't know how long he'd been there or how we'd failed to notice, but I was never so glad to see that boy in all my life.

"Enough with the interruptions!" Adolph held up his gun. "What are you going to do, Asshole? I have a gun. Now put my bag down and get the hell out of here before I litter the forest with your fat ass."

He shooed him away with the gun as though he were talking to an annoying puppy.

Sonny didn't move. "I don't think you want me to leave," he said.

"Really? And why's that?"

Javen twirled Adolph around and sent him airborne with a boot between his legs. Adolph screamed and fell, writhing on the ground with his hands to his crotch. Javen walked slowly over to him, kicked him viciously in the head and then picked up the gun and tossed it to Sonny.

Sonny bent over him. "Who else here is big enough to keep my friend from killing you very, very slowly?" But before Adolph could answer, Sonny stepped out of the way and let Javen's rage take over. With every punch and kick and spit, in my mind I screamed, *Yes! Yes! Yes!*

I tried to speak. "Antonia." I choked on my blood, spitting it out to try clearing my throat.

It scared her. "No, no, no. Don't talk. Don't talk."

"I need to tell you..."

"No! You'll tell me later!" She kissed my forehead and finally quit trying to hold back her tears.

"Javen, help me!"

"Antonia...what if there isn't a later and you never know how I feel...." I don't know if I actually said the words. I couldn't hear myself over the pounding of our hearts and Adolph's beating.

"Javen!" she yelled again.

Javen stopped and turned to Antonia and me. Watching her hold me, his face lost its anger.

Sonny held the gun to Adolph's head that now curled between his legs in a fetal position.

"You hold on, Joe. You're gonna make it," Javen said, running toward us. "We need to haul ass to Silver City, Sonny."

She continued to rock me, her warm face pressed against my cold one. The pain was finally gone. I felt nothing, not even the pressure of her hand on my wound. I just felt relief. Antonia was safe. They'd saved my girl.

"Let's go," Antonia said reassuringly. She kissed my lips for the second time, staining hers red. "You're gonna let me hear that poem later. Promise me."

I didn't want to make a promise that I might not be able to keep. But I didn't want her to be afraid anymore, either, and so I nodded my head and smiled, slowly surrendering to the sleepiness as I felt my body being lifted.

I took one last look at Antonia before shutting my eyes.

Chapter 5
Sonny's Story

I'd had it with Javen. He was supposed to be my best friend, but all I ever got from him was bullshit. I wasn't his friggin' sidekick. I thought about how I could tell him this as we walked around the outside of camp looking for Joey and Antonia. If I hadn't been so drunk I think I might've just told him to go to hell. My head felt the way a CD must feel after a half-hour of spinning. I wanted to hurl again just thinking about it, but I knew it would only add to Javen's attitude, so I tried my hardest to hold back.

Freakin' Javen. If his Mom wasn't such a bitch and his dad a Class A dickhead, I don't know that I would've tolerated him the way that I did. But, deep down, I knew that underneath his muscle shirts, the Playboy bunny tattoo on his back, his foul mouth and the pissed-off look on his face, there was just a scared kid who didn't like to admit that he needed us. Javen was all right. He showed his appreciation in his own way. He was always trying to set me up with chicks, always helping out at the house with the yard and my room, stuff like that. And he loved it when one of my sisters wanted to pick his brain when it came to their homework. I think it's about the only time he felt smart, even if the little punks were only asking him because they had a crush on him. Anyway, he didn't deserve the bullshit he got from his parents. Nobody really knew just how bad it was. Well, nobody but me. It's a wonder he wasn't worse. Javen's parents didn't beat on him or work him to death. Nah, they just pretended he wasn't there. He was like a houseplant that never got watered. I always wondered how he'd made it past the age of three months, once the new started wearing off.

But that all changed the day his mom found some maryjane in one of his pants pockets. Then it was like she needed to straighten his ass out, teach him a lesson, make him appreciate how good he had it with a roof over his head. So she threw him out on the street. "Into the real world." I think those were her exact words.

I convinced my parents to let him stay with us, which wasn't too hard. All our folks felt sorry for Jav — mine, Joe's, Antonia's...but no one else's came forward with an invitation to move in. He had nowhere else to go.

My place was the best for him, anyway. I always associate a house that smells of food cookin' with family. Jav's house never smelled of food in a pot or in the oven or even on the grill. There wasn't the smell of homemade tortillas wafting from the kitchen like at Antonia's, or fresh garlic, cilantro, and sautéed onions like at Joey's, or even the smells of barbecued meat like at mine.

The Goretti house might'a been chaotic, messy, small and sappy, but it was never dull. Dad was like a circus clown, pot-bellied and full of stupid jokes. "Hey, Jav, have you heard the one about Sitting Bull?" It was embarrassing. He was allowed to make Indian jokes because he was Navajo, but God forbid anyone else try.

And then there were my four sisters, filling every corner of the house with noise. From Angie's constant piano practice rattling on in the background, to Zoë's obsession with imitating Kermit the Frog, there was no way a person could think straight, much less find a quiet space to stop and feel sorry for himself.

Still, it didn't take much for Javen to get outta hand. Like today, with the hitchhiker. Then five minutes later he's trying to make it right. So I'd forgive him. We all would. But this time I'd had it. I decided that I had just enough of a buzz left to try talking sense into him.

"Javen, Buddy, we need to talk about this shit."

He put his finger up to his mouth. "Do you hear that?" he whispered.

We stayed real still, but all I heard was the party we were missing out on, on account of Javen's headhunt.

It hadn't been two seconds into that thought that we heard a gunshot, then another. Me and Javen looked at each other and, without another word, we followed it fast. We slowed down as we heard Antonia scream, "Why? Why are you doing this?"

We never in a million years expected to see what we saw. I held Javen back when he saw a naked Dolores with a hole in her head and Antonia holding Joey's bloody body in her arms. It was unreal, more than I could handle. I wanted to run away from it. I'm ashamed to admit it, but the thought of doin' somethin' to help didn't even cross my mind.

Luckily, Javen had his head screwed on straight.

"Are you sobered up now?" he hissed into my ear.

I was, but he didn't wait for my answer.

"All right, Sonny, you see that bag over there?" He pointed to a duffel bag that lay beside Dolores. "You're gonna go get that so he'll be distracted. I'll take care of the rest."

"Javen, the dude has a gun."

"And?"

"Javen, the dude has a gun!"

He smacked me on the forehead and pointed to Joey and Antonia. "Look at them, Sonny!" he whispered. "Don't you dare be a chicken-shit right now! I need your help! I can't do this without you!

"Now, I said I'd take care of it, didn't I? So just trust me and go get the fucking bag!" He shoved me in the bag's direction.

One thing I had to give Javen...he was brave. I, on the other hand, was a chicken-shit. Class A. Maybe not always. But at this moment...hell yes I was. I didn't know what he was doin', but I knew I couldn't just watch. So I went. I crouched next to Dolores and then I grabbed it. I was one drop away from pissing my pants, but I kept my cool as I watched Javen move through the trees like moonlight. I thought, *Why can't I freakin' be like that? I've gotta be like that! I've gotta sprout some balls for Joey. For Antonia. For Javen. For poor Dolores over there.*

But I just couldn't. I didn't have it in me. And then Javen shot me his evil eye. So I did the only thing I could think to do, I pretended I was Javen. *I am Javen standing next to Dolores' dead body. I am Javen holding that piece of scum's duffel bag. I am Javen waiting for that low-life piece of shit to turn around and look me in the eye and dare to shoot me.*

Then the asshole did the wrong thing and insulted me! *Fat ass?* The dude was actually shooing me away! I didn't have to pretend to be Javen anymore. I was pissed off enough for Santino. But before I could say more than a few words to him, Javen had him on the ground and was tossing the gun to me. It all happened so fast! Soon Javen was trying to help Antonia lift Joey as I held a gun to the dude's head.

"What do we do with this guy? And what the hell do we do with her?" I asked, pointing down at Dolores. "Man, she's dead! I can't freakin' believe she's dead!" I had one foot propped on the dude's back, both hands tight around his pistol as I tried to control my freak-out.

"You kill that son-of-a-bitch, Sonny!" Antonia screamed at me through a squall of tears.

Javen knelt down by Dolores and draped his jacket over her body. Then he turned to Antonia.

"Are you hurt?" Javen asked her.

"No! It's Joey. He needs to go to the hospital *right now,* Javen!" She shook like my diabetic Mima when she needed her insulin shot.

Meanwhile, Eddie and Tommy had finally shown up after hearing the gun shots. "We can't move her. This is a crime scene now. Me and Tommy can stay here and wait for the cops while you guys get Joey and Antonia out of here."

"We're gonna stay here? Just us and Dolores? And this guy?" Tommy said, pointing a long, shaky finger at the asshole. It was good to know I wasn't the only wuss in the forest.

"Give me your jacket, Sonny!" Antonia yelled.

I carefully took it off, one arm, then the other. *Don't drop the gun, and don't point it anywhere but down.* I handed it to Eddie, who handed it to Antonia. I watched as she reached for it, blood dripping down her arm. She took her hand off of Joey's stomach just long enough to get my jacket and wrap it around him. So much blood. I'd never seen so much blood before. I couldn't believe this was happening to him. To us. We were inner-tubing a few hours before. Everyone was getting sunburned and sauced, eating 'til there wasn't anything left to eat but the bottle caps littered all over our campground.

Eddie took Joey's head, Tommy his legs. Antonia kept tight around his stomach as they ran with him back to the Suvee. I watched them until I couldn't see them anymore, then I looked down to the place where they'd just been sitting. That's when I saw my sunglasses. Smashed. Ruined. Like this trip. I couldn't help wondering if their scavenger hunt for my sunglasses played a part in this mess.

"We'll be right behind you," Javen shouted.

He was about to relieve me from gun duty, when the dude's foot was up in my crotch and the gun was fallin' outta my hands.

I fell over from the pain. Meanwhile, the dude went for the gun at the same time that Javen did. Javen won the race, but not before the dude got away.

Javen ran after him as I sat on my knees, recovering from the shockwaves.

He was back before the pain went away, looking in every direction like someone who'd lost his compass.

"Sonny, what the fuck happened?"

I looked down at the ground where the psycho had just been lying, where my foot had been holding him down about three minutes before. But there wasn't anyone underneath my foot anymore.

"What the fuck happened?" he asked again, louder this time, the gun shaking in his hand.

My fingers ached. I stretched them out, popped my knuckles, stood up and panicked. I was sure Javen would hit me when I answered, "I don't know."

But he didn't.

"What do we do now?" I asked.

"We go with Antonia and Joe, of course."

"We're just gonna leave this guy out here?"

"Yup," he answered, almost before the question was out of my mouth.

"Yeah, but —" Before I could finish, Javen had my arm and was yanking me in the direction of camp. Other curious idiots were showing up, which was a good thing. Javen told them to stick around 'til Eddie and Tommy got back. "Don't fucking leave! And don't touch her body!" he yelled at them, to make sure they knew he meant business.

We ran to catch up with Antonia and Joey, but I couldn't help from lagging behind. And it wasn't my weight or my blood-alcohol level, either. I just couldn't help thinkin' about how I'd just let a rapist and killer get out from under my size twelves. And what was up with Javen not making me feel like shit for it? The fact that he was letting it go made it all that much worse inside. Was this some sort of reverse psychology shit?

When we reached the Suvee, he pulled me aside and whispered, "Not a word of this to Antonia. We aren't gonna tell her the asshole got away until later, all right?" I nodded my head. Antonia was waiting in the back seat with Joey in her lap. She was still crying buckets, still trying to stop his bleeding with her hand.

Eddie and Tommy were waiting for us, but left when Javen yelled at them to get back to Dolores.

"Let's go!" Javen shouted at me while getting into the driver's seat.

But I couldn't.

"No. You go. There's something I've gotta find."

He was through being nice to me. "Sonny, get in the fucking car!"

But I couldn't.

"Sonny, we don't have all day!" Antonia yelled.

"It's just...."

But Javen wasn't gonna let me explain. That would've meant telling her that we lost the dude. So he flipped me off and peeled out, leaving a trail of dust for me to choke on.

Chapter 6
Antonia's Story

Joey's blood covered my left hand like a tight-fitting glove. I peeled away at the crimson-colored layer, scraping it out from beneath my manicured fingernails as the doctors put cold things on my body and asked questions I couldn't answer because they seemed too far away to hear. Their voices were just as monotonous as the police's. Both of these professions required pens, teeter-tottering pens. Taking notes without looking up, they both had a way of speaking to me condescendingly, too. One probably got paid a gazillion times more than the other by carrying a stethoscope instead of a gun. These are the kinds of strange thoughts that ran through my head as they probed me.

Between the echoes of their voices and the hospital's alcohol-scented interior, I could hardly control my urge to vomit. I'd been sitting under a microscope too long, surrounded by people I didn't know and cared nothing about. The more I sat, the more I felt a swaying motion all around me, like the inside of a baby's cradle, slow to the point of being dizzying. I wanted to unzip my skin, like the sleeping bag rolled up in the back of my Suvee, and just crawl out.

Thankfully, once they'd decided that I was going to be okay, they allowed me the freedom to walk around while waiting for my mother, God, and a miracle to arrive.

Lucky for me, Javen was brought back from the police station before the Diaz family got there.

I crouched down in a corner and watched as Javen approached them, watching his mouth move without understanding the words. Javen The Driver had now designated himself as The Explainer. He spoke to the police. He spoke to a newspaper reporter. He spoke to Joey's parents. I watched as he went out to the Suvee and came back with the gun for the police just before he'd left with them. I heard bits and pieces of this and that, his vague description of Adolph, his directions to the camp where Dolores' body still lay, his choppy explanation about why I was so speechless.

Speechless. Along with everyone else — the police, Joey's parents — he tried speaking to me, too. But I really couldn't hear.

And so I paced. I rubbed my forehead roughly, as though the tension would help me remember something important. All the while, I cried quietly, letting the tears flow unwiped down my cheeks, down the contours of my jaw and neck.

I whispered a prayer to St. Anthony I had taught myself, something I found on a piece of paper folded up in my mother's bible:

And perils perish; plenty's hoard
Is heaped on hunger's famished board.
Let those relate, who know it well,
Let Padua of her Patron tell...

Over and over, I prayed. Pleading to God, pleading to St. Anthony. Just pleading.

A nurse walking through the waiting room squeezed my shoulder, bent, and whispered, "We have to have faith."

Faith. Keep the faith. We gotta have faith. Faith. I smiled. Madrid used to say her faith was clean, my faith was pretty, Mama's faith was round. Faces...faith. Faith. It was a foreign word, as scant and obscure as the prayer I chanted. Yet I continued to pray.

Javen tapped me on the shoulder. "Antonia, your mom is here."

"And perils perish; plenty's hoard, Is heaped on hunger's famished board. Let those relate who know it well, Let Padua of her patron tell..."

It wasn't 'til I saw her standing in the entranceway, eyes swollen from crying and shivering in her pajamas as she caught sight of me at the exact moment I did her, that I laid my prayer to rest.

"Amen."

"Mi'ja," her lips mouthed as she opened her arms and ran toward me. I didn't meet my mom halfway. My body felt too weighed down to move. I collapsed in her arms, and she cradled me in a way that only my mother could. We cried as though we were the only two people in the room, like two abandoned babies.

I rested my head on her shoulder and took big, heaving breaths.

"Are you okay?" she whispered.

"No," I whispered back.

Mama led me to a chair and sat me down. She knelt in front of me, grabbed both my hands and looked me straight in the eyes. "Tell me where it hurts. Tell me what I can do," she said. It was *déjà vu.* My mother kneeling down to my eye level, grabbing my hands and asking me what was wrong. *Where does it hurt?*

Then again, this is who she was. I loved that about her. She wasn't interested in how it happened, like some parents might have been. She wasn't interested in finding out who was responsible, who she could blame for the whole mess. She only wanted to know how she could fix it.

"I can't leave Joey, Mom," I said, wiping my nose with the tissue she handed me.

"Baby, I know you feel like you need to be here. But I also know that you should try to get some sleep. You can spend the whole day here tomorrow if you'd like. Why don't you rest for now?" She looked at the bloody hand she was holding and started crying again.

I hugged her head. "Okay, Mom, I'll go. But I'd like to see Joey before we leave."

She breathed a sigh of relief and looked around the room for a face that might have an answer. "Javen, Hon, do you know if Antonia can see Joey?"

"I don't think so, Ms. Pacheco. He's in the ICU. They're only letting immediate family in."

"You see, Baby? We'll come back tomorrow."

"Please, Mom." I said. "Talk to his mom and dad," I whispered as I started to cry all over again. "Please?" This was more crying than I had done in my entire life. Mom knew this.

She sighed again, more heavily, wiped my tears firmly and stood. "Wait here." My mom, the miracle-maker, delivered, just as I knew she would. She came back from down the hall after a few minutes and motioned for me to follow her.

When we reached the door leading to the ICU, she said, "You don't have very long. I told Mrs. Diaz five minutes at the most. You time yourself. Please don't stay any longer than you have to, okay? I'm going to call and check on your sister."

I stood at the doorway for a moment before making my presence known. It was cold and the lighting was dim. Mr. Diaz sat alone with his son, holding his hand and crying silently. Until that moment, I had been oblivious to anyone else's pain outside of my own.

Mr. Diaz. I could never call him anything else, even if he was like the father I never had. I tried calling him José once, but it felt sarcastic and disrespectful, like I was pretending to be a grown-up. Dad felt a little too cozy. So Mr. Diaz it was.

Over the years, I had shared many meals with their family. And he had shared many stories with me, about their family in Mexico, relatives, their history, things I knew nothing about, things I envied and clung to as though they were a part of my own ancestry. He was a hard-working man, gone quite a lot, but he treated me like a daughter when we were around each other. He knew I didn't have a father. He knew I didn't have family aside from my mother and sister. I think he tried to compensate for that. He was a good man, one of the few my mother trusted. This was the first time I had ever seen him cry.

I was comfortable enough that I could've walked into the room, thrown my arms around Mr. Diaz, and told him how sorry I was, how terribly, terribly sorry I was. But my feet stayed firmly planted to the ground. *Not yet. Leave him alone with his son. An apology isn't going make him or Joey feel better.*

Then he looked up and saw me. He invited me over, waving me in as he wiped his tears with the back of his other hand. I walked in, walked over to him and hugged him tightly. I didn't apologize. I couldn't. I didn't want to utter a single word, afraid my voice might shatter what was left of his heart.

He pulled up a chair for me to sit next to him and I sat, watching Joey's chest move up and down ever...so...slowly. His eyes twitched, like he was dodging something fast-moving in the midst of a bad dream. I wanted him to wake up, if only so he would quit reliving that moment. I imagined him preparing for the bullet, dodging it before it hit him, but getting hit anyway, then reliving it again and again, trying to change the outcome each time. I couldn't stand to look anymore. My crying had been so unbelievably satisfying. It suddenly felt very uncomfortable as I tried to hold it in like I'd done so many other times before. My eyes burned. My throat hurt. My lips were chapped and quivering. Even my stomach ached for him.

And then it was as though Mr. Diaz was reading my mind. "You go right ahead and cry, mij'ita. Tal vez tu vos lo saque de su pesadilla. Maybe your voice will pull him from his nightmare."

And so I did. I hadn't needed but the simplest invitation from him to enter the room earlier and now to cry until my nasal membranes swelled shut. He was still Mr. Diaz. But if he could treat me like a daughter even at a time like this, then I felt I should act like one. I relaxed.

We sat in silence for what seemed like forever. He was the one to finally speak. "Javen told us what happened. I'm sorry you had to go through that, mi'jita."

"I didn't go through anything, Mr. Diaz. Joey and Dolores are the ones who suffered."

"No. Tú también. You are still suffering, just like his Mami and me."

He put an arm around me and I rested my head on his shoulder. We continued to watch Joey lie and twitch restlessly.

"You know," he said. "I promised mi'jo we would go fishing every summer since he was eight years old. My little boy. Maybe if I had made good on that promise he wouldn't have had to ditch school to go see that river today."

Oh, how wrong he was. If nothing else, I could let him know just how wrong he was. "I think you should know that he probably would have gone to the river today even if you had taken him fishing every single summer for the last ten years, Mr. Diaz. It was just a stupid senior tradition to ditch school right before graduation. You shouldn't blame yourself. Joey knows how hard you work for your family."

Mr. Diaz grinned pitifully, putting up that same front that I had as I'd sat there trying not to cry.

I hugged him just as Mom peeked her head through the door. "Antonia?"

"I'll be right there, Mom.

"Mr. Diaz, I know Joey probably can't hear me but...do you think...?"

"I'll be outside the door. Take your time, mi'ja."

"Thank you."

I grabbed Joey's hand and kissed it. I ran my fingers through his curly, black hair. I was so in love with him.

I gently laid my cheek on his forehead. Eyes closed, tears streaming.

"I should have told you that I loved you years ago, Joey. I should have told you how the memory of your voice could help me fall asleep at night.

"But you should know that it wasn't your words. The warmth of your breath is what drew me in."

I kissed his lips. "Now please wake up," I whispered.

I walked to the door and turned for one last look. Joey's eyes, they weren't twitching anymore! I could hardly believe what I was seeing. Was it me, his dad, or the miracle I had beckoned from God that made Joey's eyes quit twitching? He wasn't awake. He wasn't smiling. But his eyes had quit twitching.

I turned to call his dad back into the room when all the machines surrounding him began to hum loudly in unison. In an instant, I became driftwood floating haphazardly in a room that was immediately flooded with staff, bumping me roughly, their current pushing me downstream until I was finally out of the room entirely.

Mr. and Mrs. Diaz ran back toward me. Mrs. Diaz went straight to Joey, screaming his name in a way that made my teeth hurt and my skin goosebump. It was fingernails scraping a chalkboard.

Mr. Diaz hesitated by the door and looked at me in confusion.

"His eyes had just quit twitching! I...I...I was just coming to tell you! I...I...."

But he wasn't listening to me anymore. And, like so many other things, I had to just let it go. A marching band would have gone unheard in that room.

"Si hay un Dios...they will catch the person that did this to my son," he said with newfound anger.

"What?" Adolph was caught — wasn't he?

"I have to have faith, mi'ja, that they will find him," he said before shifting in the direction of his family, leaving me to wonder alone.

Chapter 7
Javen's Story

She was still crying as she walked back into the waiting room. Even with her bloody hand, her swollen eyes, her body bent with sadness and exhaustion, she was still beautiful. Even more so now. I'd never seen her like this. I'd never even seen her cry before.

"How is he?" Mrs. Pacheco asked.

She just shook her head. She couldn't speak. And I knew.

What was I supposed to say to her? Before I had the chance to give it much thought, she was walking my way, pulling me into a corner and doing all the talking.

"Why didn't you tell me?" she screamed.

"Tell you what?"

"Why didn't you tell me that Adolph got away?"

Shit. I hadn't counted on the Diaz family telling her. Actually, I hadn't thought very far ahead at all when I decided that she shouldn't know.

And then something else occurred to me. "How do you know his name?"

"That is not important! Wha-why didn't you tell me, Javen? How could you let him get away?" She was smacking me in the chest halfheartedly and crying like she was petering out.

I held her arms down and pulled her to my chest. "I'm sorry, I don't know why. I don't know how." And I didn't. I felt angry all over again just thinking about it. "Alls I know is that I couldn't tell you, not at a time like that." She finally quit swatting at me. But I knew it was only because she was emotionally exhausted, not because she wanted to quit hitting.

"Don't worry. They'll find him. *I'll* find him."

After nearly half an hour of letting things sink in and calm down, Ms. Pacheco finally walked over to us. "It's getting late. Maybe we should go.

"Are your parents coming, mi'jo?"

The answer to that was an absolute no. To tell the truth, I was kicking my own ass for even leaving a message on their voice mail. I knew they wouldn't come. What was I thinking, setting myself up for disappointment?

"Are you coming with us?" Antonia whispered. Her tone of voice had changed. I guess she was through being mad at me for not telling her about Adolph. Maybe she just realized that being angry took energy she didn't have.

"Nah, I'll just wait around here a bit longer," I said with my best don't-worry-about-me smile.

She rolled her eyes. "Don't be ridiculous, Javen."

"Seriously, what are my options, Antonia?"

"One, we take you home."

"No way." I didn't want to show up at a door that had its locks changed on my account. They knew where I was. They knew what happened, if not from the message on their voicemail, then probably from the 10 o'clock news. I was not going back there. I was already eighteen. I was graduating. I didn't need them, and they obviously didn't need me.

"Two, we take you to Sonny's place."

"No way! I'm not gonna worry those people by showing up this late at night without Sonny."

Sonny's parents. I hadn't called them yet. But what the hell was I supposed to tell 'em, anyway? I promised myself that I'd call them in the morning. Anyway, they had to have heard something from the cops already. They probably knew more than I did by now about where he was and how he was doing. For all I knew, they were already driving out there to look for him themselves.

"Fine. Then I'll just wait here with you until your parents show up."

"Just fucking go home, Antonia!" It came out before I could stop the words.

I lowered my voice and tried to start over. "I'm sorry. I didn't mean to swear. Just...quit worrying about me. I'll be fine. I want to stay. Alone."

I took off my baseball cap and sat down. I rolled it around and around inside the fists of my hands, staring at the floor beneath my feet and praying to God that He would just keep the tears in the back of my brain where they belonged. I didn't want to shed one single tear, not if they were going to believe it was for my parents. My body would use way more energy producing salt water than those two people were worth.

I put my cap back on and was about to stand when Antonia's mother sat beside me and began rubbing the middle of my back. "Are you hungry, mi'jo?"

I was. I hadn't thought about food for a very long time. Now that she mentioned it, I was pretty hungry. But I didn't answer her. I wasn't sure how to.

"What am I saying? Yes, of course you are," she said. "You're coming with us, Javen. I've decided to get a room here in town. We can go back to Santa Ana in the morning. We aren't going to worry about your parents anymore tonight. It's late; you're tired and hungry. Those are the things we need to deal with right now." She continued rubbing my back gently as she spoke.

I looked at Antonia, who seemed just as surprised at her mother's announcement. Kinda like old times.

"But —"

"No buts. I'm not *asking* you anything. I'm telling you. So go. Get your things."

"Are you sure?" The question was for Ms. Pacheco, but I directed it at Antonia.

By now, she was sitting on the other side of me with her legs pulled up toward her chest, her arms wrapped around them. She pulled off my cap and put it over her own head. "Yes, I'm sure."

It sealed the deal.

Ms. Pacheco sighed heavily. "We'll get you both fed, and when you feel up to it, maybe you guys can tell me what happened today."

"I need a minute first," Antonia said as she stood.

"Where are you going?"

"The Ladies' Room. I just need a minute alone, 'kay, Mom?"

Ms. Pacheco didn't seem to like the idea, as though it wasn't actually about her relieving herself. But she agreed anyway.

From where I sat, I could see that the cameras and reporters were heading straight for the lobby. I might not've noticed if it wasn't for the microphone that was suddenly shoved into my face by a tall, blonde woman who came out of nowhere.

"Mr. Schroeder?" she said.

I didn't answer. I was too busy wondering how the hell she knew my name. There was nothing about her that said "local newspaper." Besides, I'd already talked to all the local yokels. This woman was rude enough that, if she was a man, I might'a decked her. The fact that I didn't answer made no difference to her. She didn't care whether or not she had my permission to keep going; she was on a mission to open up my mouth with that microphone in her hand.

"Mr. Schroeder, I'm with Channel 4 news, and I was told you were at the incident in the Gila National Forest. Could you make a statement as to what exactly occurred tonight?"

As soon as the others saw that I was someone halfway knowledgeable, I was surrounded. It was like a breadcrumb dropped into the mouth of an ant hole. What shitty luck for me.

Ms. P grabbed my wrist and pulled me outside toward her car.

"What about —?"

"I'm going back in there to answer some questions for them. That way they'll leave you alone and still have something to take back to their bosses."

"But you still don't know —"

"Yes, but they don't know that," she said as she walked back. "Oh, and I'm going to check on Antonia while I'm in there." She tossed her keys to me. "I'm sorry I interrupted you. Madrid really hates when I do that."

When I got into the car, for some reason, I locked myself in, the way I'd done when I was five and my mother would go see Dad at the grocery store. I'm not sure why.

I remember she'd be in that grocery store for hours, never once coming out to check on me. One time I made the mistake of getting out. It was an emergency, though. I remember weighing out the options in my head — stay in the car and pee in my pants; get Mom really mad. Or get down, look for a bathroom, and still get Mom really mad. Either way she was going to be mad. I figured I might as well be comfortable, so I made the big trip through the motion-detecting glass doors of the grocery store. In seconds I found a bathroom and made it back before she even noticed. I thought I was hot shit until I was about five feet from the car and realized that I didn't have the keys with me. I peeked into the window, and there they were, on the driver's side seat, pretty as you please, inside a hot car with every window up and all four doors locked. I stared at those keys for what felt like three hours, in utter fear. What would she do to me? Looking back, I don't know why I was so afraid. She never hit. She never touched me at all. No, she just yelled. But she yelled at me like I was a man, a man who'd cheated on her, beat her, stolen everything she had. She yelled at me like she hated me.

I might've even been able to live with just that. But it was the rest of it that made its mark on me worse than any fist or foot ever could. She'd forget about me. Forget to feed me. Forget to put me in bed or wake me up or stick me in a tub of water once in a while.

It was never truly forgetfulness, though. I know that now. It was calculated. And it was for locking the keys in the car. It was for having pot in my pocket. But mostly, I think it was for being there.

Thankfully, though, everything worked out fine in the end. Even though Dad always ate at the deli and Mom lived off of Lean Cuisines, there was still always food in the house. Maybe that was the upside of having parents who owned a grocery store. But as long as there was stuff to eat I could take care of myself, living off of dry cereal and ice cream, or milk and bread.

Puberty was the best thing that could've happened to me. Because, the older I got, the more sophisticated my meals became. With the ability to operate a can opener and the muscle to open a jar, I could eventually add pickles, tuna, peanut butter, and even sodas to my diet.

I could go to bed when I wanted and wake up when I was ready, too. I could choose to bathe or not. Although the more I realized that women like Ms. Pacheco liked cleanliness, the more I decided it was better to be clean.

First time I ever realized that was the first day of Kindergarten. It was raining out and my mom was late picking me up. So Ms. P offered to take me home. I remember Antonia let me have the front seat. She sat in the back with her sister.

We drove to my house, but nobody was home. I had nowhere else to go, so we went back to the school and waited a little while longer. Every time a car passed, I'd perk up, then droop back down with disappointment when I'd realize it wasn't her. After everything, I still wanted my mom to be there after school.

Ms. Pacheco ended up taking me to her home that day, and many more days to come. Each time, she'd take to cutting my nails and cleaning my ears. She even gave me a haircut once.

"Good as new!" she'd say when she was all done with me, and then she'd kiss the top of my head. She was the mom I always wanted.

***

I was so immersed in self-pity that I jumped when Ms. P knocked on the window to let me know I could unlock the doors.

We sat in silence for about a minute. We hadn't said anything to one another yet about Joey dying. I didn't want to, and she obviously didn't know how.

"So, you took care of all the reporters?" I asked.

"Yeah," she said, but almost as if she didn't even hear the question. Her face had worry written all over it.

"And Antonia?"

"Well, she's not in the bathroom anymore, mi'jo. I'm sure she's just wandering around. Don't you think? Or maybe...." She was rubbing her hands together as if she was cold, despite her flannel pajama top and jeans, and the fact that it wasn't anywhere near cold outside of the hospital.

"Would you like for me to go look around?"

"No, no, Javen." She quit acting cold, but her face was still worried. "I told the nurses back in the ICU that we'd be in the car and to please let her know if they see her. She's...she's a smart girl. There are lots of people in there. It's not like anyone could hurt her with so many people around."

"Yeah, you're right, Ms. P. She's probably with Mr. and Mrs. Diaz."

"Yes, you're right. You're right." The worry started to fade a little. "We'll give her a little bit longer, wait for some of these reporters to leave. I just don't want to sit in the waiting room and take the chance of you being harassed. Not right now."

Now. The truth is that I hadn't really thought that much about now. About Dolores being gone. About Joey coming so close to being saved and then losing the fight so quickly. About Antonia seeing it all from start to finish.

Antonia wasn't physically hurt. I knew she'd be okay eventually. She had lots of people looking out for her. But the truth is that I didn't have a clue how I was going to handle the idea of life without Joey, once I got around to actually letting it sink in. Maybe Ms. P was right. Maybe I didn't need to be sitting in the waiting room just waiting on people to make me think.

"Listen, I'm sorry you're left feeling responsible for me again, Ms. Pacheco."

She looked at me with that same expression she used to get when I was a kid. She reached over and touched my hair and said, "Sweetheart, I know you can take care of yourself just fine."

It was true; I could take care of myself, *myself*.

I started thinking out loud. "It's too bad I couldn't take care of my friends as well as I take care of myself."

"I don't know what you mean," she said.

It was time to clue her in. She'd sat in the dark long enough. So to Ms. Pacheco's complete horror, I finally told her everything that had happened. Well, everything that I knew.

When I was finished, all she could do was cry.

"My God, how could I have let her go on that trip? What kind of mother would do that?" She was the one thinking out loud now.

I answered the questions for her. "The kind of mother who trusts her daughter. You didn't know any of this could happen. You don't have a neglectful bone in your body Ms. Pacheco, so don't even start thinking those kinds of thoughts.

"My mom, on the other hand...."

I don't know what my problem was. Joey was dead, and here I was thinking about my mom. Now it was me who was crying. Ms. Pacheco pulled me toward her and held me until I quit my crying and started sinking into my embarrassment. I looked around for something to wipe my face with.

She handed me a couple of tissues from her purse. When I was done cleaning myself up, she said, "There, good as new."

"Sorry about all that," I blurted out.

"You have absolutely nothing to be sorry for."

I looked out the window, through the parking lot, way beyond anything I could ever see out there. "Maybe. Maybe not," I murmured.

"What do you mean, mi'jo?"

I'd never told anyone what I was about to tell her. Not Antonia. Not Joey. Not even Sonny.

Chapter 8
Adolph's Story

*O*ne, *two, buckle my shoe.... Three, four, close the door....*

The old adage says you take deep breaths and count to ten when you're angry. But counting never did a thing for Adolph's anger. Anger wasn't the issue. Antipathy, maybe. The way one feels about cockroaches. Maybe when the cockroaches have the audacity to crawl over your dinner without fear or remorse. Maybe then it's anger. But when they slink through your life, gradually making their presence known, you aren't so much angry as disturbed, driven to thoughts of eradication. It is then that one must resort to removing them one nasty pest at a time. But even more importantly, one must do it quietly. That was where Adolph had gone wrong with number ten.

For Adolph, the act of counting was more of an analgesic than a tranquilizer. And so he counted everything, from how many miles he could walk, to how many cars passed him by, to how many stupid incubators he could take off this God-forsaken planet. He'd had many epiphanies in his life, but his first memory of one was that, if left to one's own devices, one could count and count and count...forever.

Today had been a bit more problematic than usual, although, no different in the end. He was reduced to counting yet again.

At the moment, it kept him from feeling the full-scale ache of his broken ribs, the throbbing inside his testicles, the tenderness in his face, the pain that comes with admitting defeat. Somehow, he had allowed number nine to get away. *Twice.* But he knew they'd meet again. It may not be true for everyone but, for Adolph, the third time was always a charm.

Number nine's name was Antonia. And she was the perfect addition to his collection — beautiful, aggressive, conflicted, but most of all, lonely. Although he had to laugh at her impudence, her supposition that he couldn't smell her Latin blood from the moment she feigned passing him by as though he didn't even exist, as though his platinum blonde hair simply blended in amongst the mongrels strutting around the forest. She assumed that, because her face wasn't dark, her eyes weren't brown, her hair wasn't black, that he wouldn't know the difference.

Well...she supposed wrong.

Indeed, number nine was a gorgeous creature, but her looks purported impurity more than all the others combined — deceitfulness, selfishness, abhorrence even. It couldn't be ignored.

Besides, he couldn't very well jump from eight to ten. He had to finish nine — the number of lives a cat has, the number of symphonies a composer will write before he dies, and, according to her journal, the day that she was born. It was kismet.

Finding her again would be easy because, amid the rambling dreams and the woes regarding her family dramas, she had recorded the number of animals she fed every morning, the number of miles it took to drive into town, the number of windows she had to clean last month, and the number of hours it took to get the police out there when someone had stolen their horses' hay. She had practically drawn him a map with all the booby traps and escape hatches laid out. While she was a girl who dramatized the most irrelevant of things, number nine was also a counter. And so she would have to appreciate the fact that he needed to find her.

Five, six, pick up the sticks....

He sat on a stool in one of the Forest Service's outhouses, inhaling the putrid stench of human waste deep into his lungs, trying to put number nine out of his mind for now. The sulfur-scented pile beneath him was alive with hungry things that would take a lifetime to count. So many hungry things...he could have fed them 120 pounds of chimichanga in one sitting...devoured so quickly that number ten would have been unrecognizable before she was even pronounced missing. He never did catch her name.

But it was all a moot point. They hadn't let him finish his business. They ruined a perfectly good meal for the immeasurable hungry things quickly multiplying, like the cockroaches that surrounded him everywhere he went.

Adolph took a deep breath and reminded himself that it was okay. He could accept their intrusion, their devotion, their obligation to number ten, a girl who would scarcely be missed in the world. He had it in him to be magnanimous, if only for the reemergence of number nine. And while she got away, he knew that her recent departure would only be temporary. A momentary respite from the inevitable. Like the counting.

Seven, eight, lay them —

The quiet night and his even quieter counting was rudely interrupted by the screeching of tires and the crassness of The Red Hot Chili Peppers.

The motor ran as a sniffling little boy pulled the door open, his black silhouette outlined by the lights from the pick-up behind him.

The truck's horn honked loudly, startling the boy and reducing him to tears he anxiously wiped away.

"Apúrate, Jesús!"

"I'm scared!" he wailed.

"Hurry it up or I'm leaving you here!"

The door slammed shut as he let go of it. He could no

longer see anything — the car or the lights or the man in front of him.

"What's the matter?" a deep voice said, shattering what was left of the little boy's courage. A discerning ear might have been able to hear the menace in it. But Jesús' five-year-old ears were anything but discerning. And the darkness kept his eyes from determining whether he could trust this voice or not. Instinct told him not.

And so he didn't speak. Nor did he see Adolph's smile widen.

"There's only one stall. So I'll move and you can use it, okay?" Adolph tried to disguise his grunts of pain with a cough as he slowly hoisted himself up and moved aside.

The boy didn't acknowledge his question/statement. The only sound that came from him was the chattering of his teeth.

"It's dark, so give me your hand...Jesús, is it?" Adolph said as he reached across the darkness and grabbed the boy's wrist.

Jesús pierced the air with a short, high-pitched shriek that couldn't be heard over the music blasting from his mother's stereo. But, still, he let himself be pulled to the stall that led to the hole that led to the pile of hungry things.

"Now put your hand down."

Adolph placed his hand on the rim of the stool so he could feel for himself.

"This is where you go," he said and inhaled exaggeratedly. "You smell that?"

Again, Jesús remained quiet.

"I'll bet you can." Adolph said as he inhaled deeply once more. "You smell that, Jesús?"

He knew the boy's head was nodding, even if he couldn't see it. "See, you didn't need my help. All you had to do was follow your nose to find the pot."

Jesús laughed nervously, and Adolph reveled in his victory, just as his new ride's horn honked one last time.

Nine, Ten...do it all again.

Chapter 9
Antonia's Story

I didn't understand how it could be possible. Any of it. Dolores, Joey... Adolph missing.

He'd quit the nervous twitching. I was sure that my prayers had been answered, that this was all a terrible dream holding me hostage.

Less than twenty-four hours before, we were driving down a winding road, singing, laughing, secretly aching to tell the other our deepest feelings. What robbery. I could still feel the remaining butterflies in my stomach from this morning. I remembered my hesitation, the flirtation I indulged in.... It all seemed so silly now, such a waste of time. If only I had said something sooner. If only I had told him about my feelings just a day before, a week before, a year before! Could any of this have been prevented by mere honesty? My honesty?

I sat on the toilet, reading the writing on the walls around me. *Call Dick for a good time. Jennifer M. is a bitch. Maria and Mario 4 ever.* The nausea that had been building up needed out. I stood up and hunched over the toilet. My stomach heaved violently, until what little food that was in there emptied out. I edged my way back around and tried to regain my balance.

Who are these people I wondered, not Dick or Jennifer M. or Maria and Mario. Who were the people that thought these messages were so important that they needed to share them with the rest of the world as they sat on the toilet doing their business?

I reached into my pocket and pulled out my Suvee key.

I wondered if it would work. I scratched the letter A into the wall. And then I thought about how many people came into the hospital's lobby bathroom to let off steam just as I was. Maybe they were in here for privacy. Maybe they were feeling intense emotions, and it just so happened that they were sitting on the pot. It was a long shot, but it was happening to me. And then I remembered something: my dream of the little man and the little lady with the shaky English. *He will show you the way when you're ready. In your hand is the key; use it to let him know.*

My hands. The key.

Next to the A, I wrote, NTONIA IS READY.

I waited probably five minutes for something to happen — bells, lightning, a voice from above to echo into the room, anything at all. I received nothing but the sound of toilets flushing around me, doors squeaking open and closed, faucets running, paper towels being yanked and rumpled and tossed. It depressed me further. I finally got my butt up and decided I had kept poor Javen and Mom waiting long enough.

I cleaned out my mouth and splashed cold water on my face before opening the door to leave. That's when I heard footsteps fading down the corridor. I looked in their direction and saw a man walking away. He had dreadlocks pulled back into a ponytail. He was wearing a tie-dyed t-shirt, too. I was paralyzed with fear, but only for a second. An itchy curiosity took its place, one that needed to be scratched immediately. I ran to catch up with him as he turned the corner toward the waiting room. I followed, looking from one corner of the room to the other and everywhere in-between. And then I noticed that he was leaving the hospital. He turned and looked directly at me. Once again, I froze with fear as I was now positive that this was the hitchhiker. Then he winked and gave me that grin from before. He was safe. He could be trusted. I knew this deep in my core. But what did he want? What was he doing here?

"There's an explanation for everything," Joey always said. He would want me to investigate. Mom and Javen would just have to wait a little bit longer.

I made the sign of the cross and followed him out.

I had had so many questions, but when I finally caught up to him, they all just faded into the background. And so I walked alongside him in silence. He turned to me and smiled like an old friend. I returned the smile. We walked for what felt like half a mile before I looked down at his shoes, barely serving their purpose at all. Through the holes in the tattered leather I could see that his toes were clinging to the soles for dear life.

"Are your feet okay?" I asked him.

He stopped and looked down at his feet, still smiling. "Did you know that before the 1800s shoes were not made for the right and left feet? They were just made for feet?" That's when I noticed his beautiful voice. He spoke with an indistinguishable accent. *How had I not noticed that before?*

I shook my head in disbelief of it all, but also in response to the trivia he'd just shared. It reminded me of Joey.

We continued to walk. It was probably ten minutes before I gained the nerve to say what I wanted to say.

"Sir?"

Again, he stopped walking and faced me.

"Sir, I just want to say that I'm sorry for what my friend did to you this morning."

This time he shook his head.

We hadn't been walking very fast, but already we were standing overlooking Piños Altos creek. It had a small, rare stream of water flowing through its creek bed, shadowed by pines that smelled as bold as I had felt just the day before. He walked down to it, I thought for a better look. But he laid his backpack down gently, bent over with cupped hands and began to drink thirstily.

I watched him like a guiltless child watches a lamed

animal dying, without a sense of shame for not helping. I was awed by this simple, mysterious man, allowing me the opportunity to get close. But was he even a man? Was he a ghost? A thirsty ghost? A ghost with bleeding feet and the stench of robust sweat clinging to him and his belongings?

"I really am sorry," I repeated when he was through drinking.

"What in this life has given you the sweetest feeling, Antonia?"

The fact that he knew my name sent a swift chill up my spine. That coupled with the idea that I was talking with a complete stranger made it hard to focus on his question. I had to remind myself that it was okay. I focused for a moment, closing my eyes. "The sweetest feeling," I repeated. And then it came to me. "Sleeping cuddled up next to my mother. Feeling so warm and secure, so protected, as though the world could end and it would be okay because I was with her."

Again, he grinned, wider this time, baring teeth caked in grime. "Did you know that about yourself?"

No, I hadn't. But I didn't say so.

"What do *you* think the sweetest feeling is?" I asked him.

"Many things," he answered. "Too many to count, and yet not all of them good by most people's definition."

I looked at this foreign hippie and shook my head, wanting to laugh at the absurdity of it all.

"It's okay to laugh," he said. "Be true to yourself. Always be true. You've learned that recently, yes?"

"What do you mean?"

"Your friend. Had you been true to yourself, you would have shared your feelings for him sooner. You may have learned he felt the same way sooner. You may not have prevented his accident, but you may have had more time together, yes?"

"How do you know these things?" I asked.

"Let's sit," he said.

I sat down, and I wasn't afraid or the least bit apprehensive. I was only curious.

"Have you heard of the Rosetta Stone?"

I had. From Joey, actually. "Yes, it's the stone that was
used to decode the Egyptian hieroglyphics."

"That's correct!" he said. "The reason it was possible to
decode the hieroglyphics is because it had two languages
with which to cross reference the text..."

"Egyptian and Greek."

"Right again. The Rosetta Stone served as a key to
understanding. It demystified and taught...a lot like your
friends, your family, and —"

"My memory," I finished.

He smiled. "Yes. Your memory.

"What did you learn today, Antonia?"

"Learn?"

"Yes, what did you learn?"

"Well...I learned that I shouldn't talk to strangers."

He wasn't pressed against my shoulder. He wasn't flirting. But he grabbed my wrist. And it was okay. "You and
me — we are not strangers, though, are we?" he said.

"I know," I said to my own surprise. But we were
strangers. So why didn't he feel like a stranger?

"I'll ask again. What did you learn?"

"I learned...I learned that my friends are brave."

"What else?"

"I learned that I am brave, too."

"And?"

"I learned...that crying feels good."

"What about your family?" he asked me.

"My family?"

"Yes, what did you learn about your family?"

"I learned how grateful I am for my mom."

"What about your sisters?"

"What?"

"What did you learn about your sisters?"

Sisters. Sisters. I looked into his golden brown eyes, so deep I felt as though I could see past my own reflection in them. My dream — my many dreams — flashed in them like a fast-moving film. I watched, entranced, engrossed, enduring pain in my heart, pain like... like watching a little girl lying in bed dying. *Save me, O God! I heard in my own head. For the waters have come up to my neck. I sink in deep mire, where there is no standing; I have come into deep waters, where the floods overflow me. I am weary with my crying; my throat is dry; my eyes fail while I wait for my God.*

I couldn't see anymore. My eyes filled with tears. My sisters. My sisters.

"What should you do, Antonia?" he asked me.

"I don't know!" I screamed. "Can you help me?"

"You asked me to show you the way. That I can do. You must do the rest."

"But I don't know how!"

"You talk about your mother, Antonia. But there is someone else. There is someone else you always seem to forget."

I tried to control my crying long enough to think for a moment.

"Madrid?"

He smiled and squeezed me with his warm hand. "Go to her. She has always been there to help. All you need do is ask. Your mother has always provided the sweetest feeling for you. But you will never feel anything quite as sweet as the exposition of the truth. Just remember it will not necessarily feel good to begin with."

I stood and had the most desperate need to run. Not out of fear but out of urgency, and impatience.

"It's okay. Make haste, my beloved."

I turned to run, but before I started he called, "Antonia."

"Yes?"

"Always remember that feeling you get when you are

lying cuddled next to your mother. Always remember how she has made you feel — how loved and protected you are. Everything she does for you in this life is out of love and devotion."

I smiled and turned to sprint. I was across the creek when I realized that I hadn't even thanked him.

I turned back, but he was already gone.

After arriving back at the hospital, I searched the entire bottom floor before checking for them out in the parking lot. As I approached Javen and my Mom sitting together in her car, Javen turned to her, hugged her tightly and kissed her cheek. But I didn't have time to wonder what that was all about. I was preoccupied with thoughts of Madrid.

Chapter 10
Javen's Story

My mother was raped." When the words came out, it was like I'd taken out a long hair that had been stuck in the back of my throat. *Amazing.* Four small words, and that hair was finally out.

But Ms. Pacheco didn't get what I was saying.

"What?" she asked.

And so I repeated myself.

Maybe it was the fact that I said the words with the same tone I used when ordering a salad at a restaurant or explaining to a barber what I wanted. She just wasn't getting it.

"My dad. He isn't my real dad. Did you know?"

It took a minute, but she nodded.

"You know?" Now I was the one who wasn't getting it.

"Javen, I'm not so sure we're talking about the same things," she said.

"Then let me just spell it out. My mother was raped. By some Mexican. Eighteen years ago. Doesn't it make sense? Look at my skin! Look at me! Not only that, I'm angry; I'm violent; I'm mean. Isn't that what everyone says?" I was on a roll. "And why the hell not? I'm the son of a rapist. That's why my parents hate me. That's why they didn't come last night, and that's why they won't be at my graduation."

I needed to disconnect now, before I got outta hand. I picked up a booklet of CDs from the floorboard and began flipping through them.

Ms. Pacheco turned to face me and gently pulled the

book away, placing it on her lap. "Javen, you listen and you listen good. You are not, and I repeat, *not* the product of rape. I don't know where you got your information, but it's very wrong."

I had to laugh. "It's okay, Ms. Pacheco. You've been nothing but nice to me, but it's really okay. I know the truth. And besides all that, you weren't even living here when I was born."

"That's true, but...." She couldn't complete her sentence. What else was there to say?

"I know the truth, Ms. P. I heard it from my own mother."

Ms. Pacheco's eyes narrowed. "What exactly did she tell you?"

"She didn't tell *me* anything. It's what I heard her tell my dad a long time ago."

I'd already said enough. I pulled the CD case back onto my lap and tore the Velcro closure open with a loud rip. "Do you mind if I stick something in while we wait?" I asked without looking at her.

"Javen!" She pulled the case away again and this time threw it into the back seat. I wasn't getting off as easily as I'd hoped. But it was my own fault for opening my big mouth in the first place.

"I want to know exactly what you heard," she said.

My eyes wanted to fill with tears again, but this time I harvested them up faster than I did the weeds in Sonny's back yard. I clenched my jaw and conjured up that long-ago memory.

"I was eight years old. It was my birthday." I laughed. "They'd actually thrown me a party once upon a time. Antonia was there." I looked over at her. "Do you remember?"

"Perfectly," she said. "That was the one and only party she ever attended in your honor."

I laughed again. "Yeah, that would be the one. Anyway, do you remember anything special about that party?"

She didn't answer.

"Like, maybe that you all were celebrating without me?"

Ms. Pacheco smiled uncomfortably and nodded her head.

"She told you all I peed my pants, didn't she? She probably said that I was really embarrassed, and that's why I wasn't coming back out."

"That's not what happened?"

"Yes and no. I *did* wet my pants, but it wasn't embarrassment keeping me away." I closed my eyes, but the image of that day wouldn't go away. Maybe it was because I wouldn't let it.

"Right before the party, my parents were arguing. My dad told her she'd 'spent way too much money on the little bastard.' He started in on her about how she had better get her priorities straight or she could take her little bastard and get the hell out of his house. 'Why do you punish me for being raped?' she said.

"I didn't know what that word meant. I didn't even get that the conversation was about me. It was during the party itself; that's when I realized. I remember she had one of the neighbor's kids on her lap. She was clapping his hands together and laughing. I walked over to her and asked her why she treated other kids better than she treated me. I reminded her that this was *my* birthday.

"That's when she said, 'I choose my friends. Unfortunately, I've inherited you.' When I started to cry, she put the kid down, grabbed my wrist, pulled me off to the side and whispered into my ear, 'This is your last party, do you understand me? I didn't go through all this trouble for you to start crying! You're dad isn't even on speaking terms with me! I am *sick* of suffering with you all alone, sick of your ungratefulness.' She shoved me off when she was done venting and, as I walked away, she said loud enough for everyone to hear, 'Now make Mommy's life a little easier and go play with the nice kids. Quit being such a baby.'

"That was the day I realized that it wasn't just my imagination."

"What wasn't your imagination, Javen?"

"They really didn't love me." Jeez, I'd taken this to a completely unexpected level. "Anyway, the next thing I know, I'd wet my pants and was running to my room to camp out under my bed. I didn't come out 'til the next morning."

"The next morning?"

"I could'a stayed there longer, but I got hungry."

Ms. Pacheco looked angry. She even made a low growling sound as she rolled up her sleeves. If I didn't know any better, I'd'a said she wanted to hit me. But then she started to speak.

"When we first moved to this town, mi'jo, I was a substitute teacher. At that time your mother was an aide for Mrs. Mondragón, the fifth grade teacher at Cooper Elementary. That was the year that Mrs. Mondragón was having her baby. I substituted for her class the entire time she was on maternity leave. Your mother was one of the first acquaintances I made in this town. She didn't have too many friends of her own. In retrospect, I understand why. But, anyway, she confided things in me..."

"Like what?"

She took a deep breath like she was going under water.

"What is it, Ms. Pacheco?"

"You're right. Steve isn't your father. But your mother wasn't raped, Javen. Your real father's name is Margarito Gutierrez. She was having an affair with him. She thought she was in love with him. She told him she was going to leave Steve, but evidently Margarito didn't share her feelings. He was a migrant worker, mi'jo, and when that last crop had been harvested, he moved on to the next small town and she never saw him again. Can you imagine? Melinda Schroeder, rejected by a migrant!

"*Then* she found out she was carrying his baby. You." She reached over and squeezed my hand. "Steve had to have known about the affair. Apparently, the whole town knew. But she tried, and probably still tries to this day, to make him believe she was raped by some nameless, faceless Mexican. I'm sure it's easier for her to pretend that she was raped than to admit she was rejected by a charming, incredibly handsome migrant nobody, someone she claimed she loved if only for the amount of time it took for her to end up pregnant.

"But it was never really love, Sweetheart. She could never treat you the way she has if it had been. Believe me, I know. Either way, it wasn't rape. I'm sure your biological father was a decent, hard-working man who's only crime was not loving the married woman he probably never even knew he impregnated! I'm also sure he would have tried to be a part of your life if he'd known about you. And you know what, maybe he *still* would."

I didn't know what to say. I was in shock.

"Are you okay?" Ms. Pacheco finally asked when she got the nerve to speak again.

I could tell by her face that she was feeling bad, either for telling me in the first place, or for never telling me before today. I had to let her off the hook.

"His name was Margarito? You didn't just make that part up?"

We both laughed.

I was the one who was actually let off the hook. There weren't evil genes hidden in my DNA after all. Hell, I could be outwardly sweet, even happy, if I wanted to.

I hugged Ms. Pacheco tightly, even kissed her cheek.

And then, just like that, the sadness was back. I looked up and saw Antonia and remembered that Joey was dead.

***

She never did explain where she'd been or what had taken so long. And we didn't ask. It didn't even matter anymore. She said she was finally ready to go to the police station and make a statement. For some reason, she wanted to talk to Madrid, too... right now. She said she didn't care about eating.

Ms. Pacheco, who normally gives her what she asks for, put her foot down. It was late; she could visit with the police in the morning, but right now she needed food and sleep and to talk to *her* about what happened.

But she didn't want to talk it over with her mom...or me for that matter. So it was complete silence as Ms. Pacheco drove us to the hotel.

We sat down at our table in the hotel room. I ate Funyuns, Twinkies, a packaged ham and cheese sandwich, and drank root beer; Antonia ate some more licorice and drank bottled raspberry tea. Quick-shop food was nearby, and the only thing we could get this late in the day, or early in the morning as it was.

Everyone was silent for the rest of the night. Ms. Pacheco never forced conversation. She knew it was too soon. "You really should try eating more," she told Antonia as she sipped from her bottle of tea. "You just need a shower," she suggested when Antonia examined the bottom of her arm and elbow, then walked to the bathroom to see her face in the mirror, the rim of her upper lip still marked with Joey's blood. "You just need sleep," she said when Antonia started to play with her uneaten licorice, biting off two eyes and a nose, then forcing the rest into the shape of a smile. "Maybe in the morning you can talk to me," she finally said before crawling into bed herself.

Maybe this will all go away, I thought, as I lay wide awake on my own double bed next to theirs. I thought about the Suvee still parked at the hospital and wished I had the energy to run back over there to pick up my bag with my favorite sleeping shorts, maybe one last beer to help me go to sleep.

I twisted and turned, finally deciding to get up and go outside before I woke up Antonia and her mother.

I walked out to the heated pool and sat at its edge with my legs flung inside. I closed my eyes and imagined myself chest-deep in the pool, alone with Antonia. I imagined her holding my face in her hands, kissing my eyes, my nose, my mouth. I imagined there was no Joey, no Dolores, nothing but the two of us and the sound of our bodies moving in water. I must have been smiling.

"Penny for your thoughts."

I opened my eyes and saw Antonia's reflection in the pool, standing behind me. She sat next to me, close to me, and lightly splashed her feet around in the water.

"Nothing really. I was just remembering something."

"Remembering what?"

"It's nothing." I didn't know what to say. I had to think of something. "I was just thinking about Sonny this morning and how scared he was about that hitchhiker. He got lots braver with the second guy, didn't he?"

She smiled. "You think he's okay?"

I didn't know for sure, but Adolph was in pretty bad shape. He couldn't be worth much without his gun. I finally decided that, "Yeah, he's fine," was the best answer I could give to put her mind at ease.

"So he stayed behind so he could find Adolph?"

I nodded. "Can you believe that guy?"

"He was just trying to make it right, that's all."

"Yeah, but what the hell could he have been thinking? Two people were shot!"

"God, I just hope —"

"Hey, any and everyone with a badge is out there right now." I didn't want either of us to consider the what-ifs. "I'd be willing to bet money that Sonny's already at home and in bed."

Antonia nodded, satisfied with that answer.

"Speaking of beds, what are you doing out of yours?" I asked her.

"I couldn't sleep. Actually, I didn't want to sleep. I was just thinking and thinking.... Before all of this, my dreams could be horrible, you know. I can't imagine what they'll be like after."

"What were you thinking about?"

"Do you have to ask?"

No, I didn't. Neither of us needed to rehash the night's events out loud.

I tried changing the subject. "I just thought of something stupid and irrelevant."

"What's that?"

"What about graduation? You think it'll be cancelled altogether? Or will they just postpone it?"

"I hadn't even thought about that," she said. "I was gonna partner up with Joey. I can't even imagine going through the ceremony without him. I guess I just won't do it."

"It's just for show anyway, right? I mean, it's not like they'll keep our diplomas as punishment for not being there. It's not like we didn't actually graduate. Because I don't wanna go, either." I avoided eye contact when adding, "Besides, it's not like I've got fucking family lined up to watch the event. If my parents couldn't show up today, what's the big deal about graduation, right?" I didn't want her pity. Or maybe I did.

Antonia rested her head on my shoulder. "You know, Javen, you really ought to cut back on all the fucks. It would be a lot easier to feel sorry for you without some of them," she said, splashing water at me with her feet.

"Oh yeah? Well, for your information, I wasn't looking for sympathy, Sweetheart," I said, splashing her back harder.

We splashed back and forth, making bigger splashes, harder splashes, until I jumped into the five-foot-deep water and pulled her in with me.

"You suck!" she said, rubbing her nose and turning her head sideways to drain the water in her left ear as she made her way to the shallower end of the pool.

"Only when asked," I said, following her. Even when I was tired, I couldn't help myself.

"You just need to buck up, girl."

"And you need to quit being a *jerk*," she said.

"A little water never hurt anyone. See?" I splashed her

again, this time right in the face. "It's a heated pool, for chrissakes."

She turned and started splashing back, getting closer and closer, her face turned away.

Pretty soon we were right up against one another, and we weren't splashing anymore. I touched her cheek. She was staring into my eyes, and I wanted so badly to kiss her.

"What was the deal with the hitchhiker this morning, Jav?" she asked, instantly breaking the spell.

"There was no deal."

"So what was up with you being such an ass to some helpless stranger?"

I backed further away from her. This was something that I'd never in a million years have guessed she'd want to talk about, especially not now, with everything that had happened since the morning drive. Maybe it was the topic of my being such a jerk that jogged her memory. Whatever it was, I just didn't have any answers that would satisfy her.

"Why bring up old shit, Antonia?"

"Because...."

I had one thing working in my favor. I knew she was tired, too tired to press me.

"You've been through a lot," I said. "We both have. The hitchhiker thing happened, like, a hundred years ago. It's ancient history. So you think maybe we can talk about it after we've had some sleep?"

I waded closer to her, but she quickly pulled away. "You're right. I'm sorry I brought it up."

Us being in the pool together, it never really was like *déjà vu*. Joey and Dolores were still dead. I felt my eyes burning red as if they'd been splashed with the over-chlorinated water I was standing in.

I turned to walk out of the water.

"What's the matter?" she asked.

"Nothing, I'm just tired." But she heard more than exhaustion in my voice.

"Why do you have to be that way?"

"What way?"

"Angry all the time."

"I'm not!"

"You are!"

"What do you want me to say, Antonia?"

"I want you to tell me what's wrong; what did I do wrong?"

"You didn't do anything. It's me. It's always me, isn't it?"

"Javen.... Come on, it was never you."

"What was never me?"

Antonia sighed. She hung her head, like she was suddenly embarrassed to even look at me. "Nothing. Just forget it."

I waited for a minute. Hell, I even gave her a bonus minute. But she never did spill what was on her mind.

"Why are you so mysterious?"

"I'm not mysterious."

As I walked out of the pool, I quoted a piece of her letter to her, "Do you remember this? 'I wish you were here. You and your smile, your laugh, your great sense of direction! (I'm lost in the rolling hills, and there's too many trees to find the North Star.) Anyway, I will definitely have to bring you back to this place. I'll fill you in on the rest of the trip when I get back, right after you tell me all about how you've managed to live without me for a week. See you sooner than you know. Con todo mi amor, Antonia'

"What the hell was that all about? You came back from Spring Break treating me like I was a bad disease."

She was holding her hand to her mouth, her eyes wet with tears again. I knew she didn't think I was someone who could memorize something so detailed, something written so long ago. I was no Joey. I wasn't trying to impress her so much as I wanted her to see herself through my eyes.

I turned to walk away again.

Antonia jumped out of the pool and ran to catch up with

me. When she finally did, she pulled my arm back so that I was facing her.

"Javen, how did you...? Did you think...?"

"What? Did I think what?"

She wouldn't answer.

"You think you can say what's on your mind just this once?"

But she couldn't. All she could do was apologize. Again and again.

I paced back and forth, trying to shake off my urge to cry right along with her or to put my fist into something breakable. She planted herself in front of me to stop my pacing. She grabbed my chin and turned my face toward her. Her wet body was shaking. "I'm so sorry," she repeated. "For everything. I'm sorry."

I hesitated for a second, running a hand through my hair angrily before hugging her as her quiet crying became out-of-control sobs.

"Don't cry," I told her. "I'm sorry, too. Just quit crying."

But she only cried more violently, loudly, looking for some comfort in me that obviously wasn't there.

"Javen," she said. "I feel like...I feel like I don't know how to breathe anymore."

"Shhhh. Don't talk like that. You're all right," I assured her. "Just calm down."

"How can we ever be happy again without Joey? And Dolores! God, her naked body, all that blood.... Javen, it could've been me! I was with that guy when you all were inner-tubing!" She sat on the cold cement and held her face.

I suddenly realized that I had had no business saying anything to the police. I was just as ignorant about tonight as Ms. Pacheco was.

The hardest thing to swallow was the knowledge that this was just as much my fault as it was anyone else's. None of us should have left Antonia alone, even for a second. Not today. Here I'd been hating Joey for being with her, but he was the one who saved her life while I chose to be pissed off on the sidelines, drinking everything I could get my hands on. Maybe he did want her more than me. Maybe I should've been keeping an eye out for poor Dolores; she wasn't lucky enough to have a Joey following her every move. Although I don't think anything would have kept her away from a good-looking stranger paying her attention.

I sat on the ground next to Antonia and wrapped an arm around her. "The subject is officially dropped for the rest of the night, okay? It's over. There's nothing we can do about what happened. We can't go back in time."

Her body was trembling, and she was gasping for air as she cried.

I just continued to hold her to me, tried pressing some calm onto her. "Shhhh. Everything's gonna be all right." I repeated it as many times as I thought I needed to convince her that I meant it.

"Why did he have to kill them?" Her voice was dwindling down to a whisper.

"Don't do this." I grabbed her chin just as she had done mine. I held it until she looked me in the eyes. "We have to put it away for now, Antonia." I wiped her tears with my wet hands. It was several minutes before her breathing returned to normal.

"You should try getting some sleep before daylight," I finally suggested.

"No," she said.

"Why not?"

"I'm not ready to go there."

"The room?"

"No...my dreams."

"Then we'll wait together. We can sit back in the pool. It was nice and warm in there."

"I'll be okay, Javen. Follow your own advice and go get some sleep. You said you were tired."

I looked over at her watch. "Antonia, it's three in the morning. We want to wake up early and go see about the police report, don't we?"

She closed her eyes. "I really am sleepy. I'm just afraid, Jav. That guy is still out there. After Adolph shot Dolores and Joey...he said it was me he really wanted. Now that he's missing —"

"Everything's gonna be okay. I won't let anything bad happen to you, Antonia." The words weren't even out of my mouth when I was already needing to retract them. At least the part about everything being okay. I wasn't so sure anymore. There was a tall, red cedar picket fence that separated the pool area from the dimly lit street on the other side. Nothing about it was particularly memorable, except for the spaces between the slats. Except for the face that stared at us from between them. I focused on it long enough to know that it was male and that it was Caucasian and probably over the age of sixteen. But it was too shadowed and too quick to disappear into thin air for me to figure out if he was blond or bald or bearded or Adolph. For a second I thought about jumping the fence and finding the dude, then decided that it was nothing but my imagination or a kid who freaked out when he realized I caught him staring...and why scare Antonia all over again over someone who's only a threat to the sheets that he sleeps on at night? I decided to leave well enough alone and vowed to never take my eyes off Antonia 'til Adolph's ass became the infamous grass. I stood up, pulled her up, and held her close as we walked back to the room.

Ms. P was awake and looking as worried as I'd expected. She didn't say a word to either of us, as if she feared it would only make things worse. I wondered how much she could actually hear through the closed window. After drying off, Antonia curled up next to her. But not before saying, "Thanks for being so sweet tonight. I don't say this often enough, but you are a good friend and I love you."

"I love you, too," I said. I'd waited my whole life to be able to say those words to someone.

As I crawled into bed, I thought about the guy we left out in the Gila, the one I'd never in a million years admit to loving, and wondered if he was all right.

Chapter 11
Sonny's Story

Mission "Capture the Bad Guy" had failed miserably. I'd spent the better half of the night with my balls up in my throat, scouring the Gila for some blond, bleeding psychopath, only to find out that my parents had every branch of this country's law enforcement searching the forest for *my* stupid ass.

I don't know what I was thinkin'. I didn't have a flashlight, a friend, or food, much less a car to haul this dude anywhere if and when I did catch up with him. I didn't even have the friggin' gun to protect myself from anyone or anything. And there were plenty of things out there. There were hoots and screetches, rustlings and scuttles, branches breaking, water rushing.... I felt like Ichabod Crane. Hell, I'm surprised I heard anything at all over the sound of my own heart pounding and the heavy breathing I was doin'.

To make matters worse, I was dying of thirst. It must'a been all that heavy breathing. As if I wasn't dehydrated enough from the booze that passed through me already. I was trying to figure out how to get back down to the river for a drink when I heard someone shouting my name. There aren't words to describe my relief. And yet, if you can believe it, I was disappointed. I'd wanted for my friends and family to read in the papers how I'd saved the day. Found the bad guy. Righted my wrong.

What the hell was I doin' trying to be a hero, anyway? It was as unnatural a concept as sneezing without blinking.

I was taken to the police station where my folks were

already waitin' on me. I was asked a gazillion questions while I was there....

Did I see the murder of Dolores take place?

"No."

Did I witness Joey getting shot?

"No."

Exactly how did the accused lose his weapon?

"Long story." But I explained the best that I could. I had it for awhile, then Javen took it away; I had to admit to letting the bad guy get away. I had to explain exactly how things went down exactly as I remembered it. Of course, after the initial "I'm so glad you're okay" speech, all that my folks wanted to know was what the hell I was still *doin'* out there. What in God's creation was I *thinkin*? Did I know I could have *died*? Did I know I was *grounded* for the rest of my life under their roof? Which, luckily, wasn't much longer.

Dad finally got tired of yellin' at me. He gave my shoulder a squeeze and went to bed, but my Ma...she wouldn't let up. She took turns hugging and yelling at me until I passed out. She woke me up at the crack of dawn, I suppose to see if I was still there. She just picked up where she'd left off when I'd fallen asleep on her. She might'a gone all day long if I hadn't been saved by the bell. Mom answered the phone quick before it woke anyone. It was Ms. P.

"Hi Felicia.... No, don't worry, you didn't wake anyone.... Yes. Yes, he is.... Yes, he's fine, thank God.... Uh-huh... Uh-huh...."

With every uh-huh, Mom's face was looking more and more upset. Before I knew it, she was crying and covering her mouth with her hand and looking around for a box of tissue. "Sure, I can..... Where...? Don't worry, I'll take care of it.... Okay.... You be safe.... Okay.... Bye-bye."

There was only one reason she would be crying. One reason why she didn't know how to look at me or just say what the problem was.

"Don't tell me," I said. "Joey."

"Come here, Sweetheart."

But there was no way I could cry in my mom's arms like when Mima died. I wasn't eight anymore, and I wasn't so innocent this time.

"I need to be alone," I said as I put my shoes on and walked outside.

She followed me out. "Sweetheart, I'm so sorry."

"Don't," I said before she could touch me.

"Look, we need to talk about this, Santino, but right now I have to leave for a minute. Antonia and her mother stayed at a hotel in Silver City last night. Felicia can't seem to get a hold of Madrid, who's over at her friend's. She's just worried — "

"What, that the killer guy is gonna find her?"

"No! She's worried that Madrid may have heard bits and pieces of the story and may not know that Antonia is all right. She wanted me to go to her friend Ashlin's house, where she's at right now, and tell her that everything is okay, that they'll be back home in a few hours."

"But everything isn't okay," I started to say.

"I know that, Honey. I know." She came at me again, but I wouldn't let her touch me. The last thing I wanted was more affection. Things were jacked up because of me. Everybody in southern New Mexico needed to be afraid. Even Madrid.

"I know where that girl Ashlin lives. Can I go?"

"Absolutely not. I don't want you out there."

"What do you think's gonna happen, Mom? She lives three blocks from here! It's not the forest and it's not the middle of the night!" I was yelling in that voice I get when I'm givin' it my best to not get emotional. Only this time it was for real.

I don't think my mom wanted to see me get more emotional, either. "It's straight there and back, you understand?"

"Yes, Ma'am."

In all the time me and Antonia had been friends, I'd

never spoken more than two words to Madrid. I didn't know why I was doin' this, except that maybe I just didn't want to be at home trying to muffle my anger and sadness into a pillow with my sisters listening at the door or whispering about me over their morning cereal.

All I'd ever said to the girl was "Hi, Madrid. Or "Bye, Madrid." I think once I might'a said, "See you later, Madrid."

When I pulled up to the front of the house, my instinct was to just honk the horn the way I was used to doin' when it was Javen or Joey or even Antonia that I was waitin' on. Luckily, I realized that it was dawn, and everyone was probably sound asleep in that house. So instead, I looked in the mirror to check my teeth, breathed into my hand to check my breath, pulled out my Carmex and swiped some across my lips and popped a Mentos into my mouth. I hadn't even made it to the front gate when Madrid was walking out.

I always thought Madrid was a spoiled, snotty little brat. She never answered when I said hello. She mostly kept to herself. Matter a fact, I couldn't think of anyone she was friends with outside of what's-her-face, her friend here...the girl with the bottlecap glasses and braces — God, I'd just said her name, too. Amy? Angela? Ashley? Ashlin? Ashlin! That's it. Anyhow, they were constantly hanging out in Madrid's room or out riding horses. They were like temperamental cats or somethin', acting all threatened around people, anxious, huffy, their heads together whispering.

So, like, one of my best friends had just died. I'd just let his killer get away. I'd barely survived the worst night of my life, and all I can think about as she's walking out of that brown, adobe house with the red shingles is how cute she's lookin' with her long, shiny, black hair pulled up in one of them high ponytails. Instead of pajamas, like I'd kinda anticipated, she was wearing a short, denim skirt and a purple t-shirt that said "Girls Rule" on the front. Madrid was tall like her sister, but a little on the curvy side like her Mama. Not fat, by any means! Just a little more shapely. I couldn't figure out when she'd turned into such a little hottie.

I stood there in front of her, not knowing what to say. "Hi, Madrid," finally came out, probably a little more enthusiastically than was necessary.

"Hi," she said back to me, probably for the first time in her life.

"I didn't expect you to come out that door before I even had the chance to knock. Did you know I was coming?"

She nodded.

"How?"

She didn't answer, which I should'a expected. I guess I was trying to press my luck. We stood there in silence for the longest minute of my life. Part of me was waiting for an answer. Part of me didn't know exactly how to say everything that needed saying. I couldn't remember the last time I'd put so much effort into talking to some girl. I mean, it was fine with me...sorta. To not wanna know about Antonia, though — I suddenly felt kinda pissed that she wasn't sayin' anything! But the chicken-shit in me that didn't like to raise dust just decided to let it go and move on.

"Well, anyhow, your mom said she couldn't get a hold of you and asked that we come by and tell you that..." But I stopped because she had grabbed my arm.

And that's when I noticed. Her mouth was open and something was tryin' to come out.

"I... I... I... I knew you were coming be-be-because your mom just c-c-c-called, Santino."

Madrid stuttered when she was a little kid. I knew that. But lots of little kids stutter. I never thought nothin' of it back then. But the older she got, the more she kept to herself and the less I heard her speak. Could it be that I just wasn't payin' attention? Because all these years she'd evidently still been stuttering and I was none the wiser! No wonder she didn't talk much! It all made sense now. I felt like such dog shit for the attitude I was working up over *her* attitude, not just today but all those other times I thought she acted high and mighty.

Once I got past the fact that she still stuttered, I couldn't get past the fact that she knew my real name. I was the one who was speechless now. I wanted to slap myself when she looked down, like she was embarrassed. That's when I noticed she had a notepad and pen in her hand. Although she should'a known it would be too hard to read unless the ink glowed in the dark 'cause the sun was still half asleep.

But suddenly everything made sense.

"I'm sorry, Madrid," I said. "I'm just a little shocked because I didn't know you knew my real name. Not too many people call me Santino."

She lifted her head back up and smiled. Maybe she was happy that I didn't make an issue of the fact that she stuttered. Maybe she just smiled because she felt like it. I didn't know or care. As usual, I just kept goin'.

"So, since my Mom got a hold of you, she probably already told you everything you need to know, huh?"

"No. She j-j-just said you were c-c-c-coming over."

That woman. Why'd she bother calling her if she wasn't gonna finish the job?

"C-c-c-c-can we sit in the van?" she asked.

"Sure! I'm sorry I didn't think of it. It is kinda chilly out," I said while running over and opening the passenger-side door for her.

We sat there for a few minutes, neither one of us talking. "Is th-th-th-there a light in here?" she finally said while holding up her notepad.

I felt like such a dumbass as I fumbled to turn the damn thing on.

"Sorry about that."

Don't be, she wrote. *I'd like for you to be able to read my notepad; I don't expect you to read my mind.*

She was nothin' like I thought she was. Nothin'.

I think Ashlin's dad was online last night, probably why Mom couldn't get through.

I laughed. "A late-night surfer, is he?"

She smiled sheepishly and nodded.

But I did talk to my mom. She must have tried one last time after talking to your mom. She called back, but you had already left. Anyway, she told me about Joey. I'm so sorry. Madrid looked up from her notepad, her brown eyes puddled up with tears. It broke my heart. Before I knew it, I was reaching over to offer her a hug. She reached her arms around me before I even realized what she was doin'. She smelled of fuzzy peaches, so good I had to inhale, stop to breathe, then inhale some more. I couldn't even tell you if I hugged her back, I was so surprised by her reaction.

"I'm so s-s-sorry for you," she whispered. I felt worse for her than I was feeling for myself. And Joey was my boy.

When she finally let me go, I tried to change the subject. "Can you believe we were supposed to be graduating tonight? I'm thinkin' it ain't happening." After saying it, I realized that I hadn't changed the subject at all.

Madrid didn't say a word. And then I suddenly got a wild hair up my butt.

"You wanna go for a ride with me?" I asked her.

She nodded again, quicker this time. I was real happy she said yes and, at the same time, wondering if Mom would send the law out lookin' for me again.

Just out of curiosity, I cruised by the football field, where graduation rehearsals were supposed to be taking place in a few hours. It was completely empty. There weren't chairs set up, a podium, a stage, nothing. In fact, the sprinklers were still going strong. A young couple was already jogging around the track.... Just another day in paradise for some folks. I wasn't in any mood to celebrate graduation, anyway. I couldn't imagine ever wanting to celebrate anything again. But passing the field and seeing life go on like normal — I don't know why, but it bothered me. I guess I wanted to see people feelin' and lookin' as sad and shitty as I did, and yet I also wanted Santa Ana to still recognize we were the latest batch of seniors being sent off into the world. I wanted to see the chairs, the podium, the stage. It would have been a tribute to Joey, even if nothing actually took place this weekend.

I pulled the family van over and cried for the first time since I got the news. I was wishing we'd never driven to the Springs, wishing there'd never been such a thing as Senior Ditch Day.

Poor Madrid didn't know what to do for me. For a minute, though, she didn't even exist, being as I was so caught up in my own sadness. And anger. I was more pissed at myself now than ever before. For losing those sunglasses that my best friends figured they needed to find for me. For losing a killer that was so unbelievably busted it was pitiful. And then for not gettin' him while the gettin' was good.

I got out, grabbed some rocks from outside the fence and started chucking them at the field. When that didn't vent my anger I started kicking my tire. I wanted to break somethin'. I went to the back of the van and got out my tennis racket.

"What a stupid tradition! What the *hell* were we doing out there on the last day of school?" I yelled as I hammered that racket into the fence over and over until I was winded beyond restoration.

"Stop!" Madrid cried. It's what finally made me snap out of it. I turned to look at her and she was shaking somethin' awful. I'd scared her.

"God, what am I doing? I didn't mean to lose it like this. I'm sorry."

She came toward me, wrapped her arms around me and buried her face in my chest. "Are y-y-y-you going to be okay?"

I thought about the question before giving her a straight answer. "You know what? I'd feel a lot better if I could just find the guy who did this."

She was so soft and fragrant. She'd instantly transported me to a whole other planet. It's weird how a person's emotions can change from one second to the next, how sometimes one extreme can change into another. It reminded me of my Mima's funeral. Feelin' like I was dying of sadness, then suddenly hearing grandpa accidentally let one loose during the eulogy. And just like that, I was hysterical with laughter.

I don't know, maybe it was apples and oranges. I couldn't think much more on it because a horn honking at us interrupted our hug and my thoughts.

It was Tom and Ed. Eddie got out of his truck and came up to me first, holding out his hand. He looked at the fence and the racket I'd thrown down. "I guess you heard then, Cabrón...."

I nodded my head. "Simón," I said quietly.

I could tell by his awkwardness he wanted to give me a hug, but the macho in him would only allow him to pat my back and give my head a rough rub. Tom didn't say a word.

"I'm glad we found you, Bro. I wanted to tell you what happened after you guys left," Eddie said.

"I don't wanna talk about it right now, man," I said back.

"No, you have to hear this, Dude," Tom chimed in.

"What is it?"

Eddie started it off. "I took it upon myself to be in charge, right? So I started by telling all the girls to go home." He pulled a cigarette from behind his ear and a lighter from his back pocket. He lit it up, took a long puff and blew the smoke up above his head before continuing. "Of course, nobody wanted to split up or leave. People were freaked, you know? Anyways, I assigned Tommy and me the job of looking for El Pinche Buey."

"El Buey?" I repeated.

"You know, the dude that killed Joey and Dolores." At the mention of their names, Eddie made the sign of the cross.

"The rapist, the sick fuck!" Tommy threw in sarcastically.

I punched Tom in the shoulder hard enough to make sure it got his attention.

He looked over at Madrid and nodded his head to let me know he got it.

Eddie went on. "Anyways, I was like Tom. I mean, I didn't wanna sit with no dead body, especially when the dead body was someone I knew, right? So I promised a case of Bud to anyone and everyone who would."

"And of course every guy there with half a set of balls went and set up a new camp over by Dolores," Tommy added.

"That left you out, Bro," I said.

But before Tommy could strike back, Eddie kept goin' like he hadn't even heard us. "Pobrecita Dolores. I told 'em it wouldn't be long before my dad got there anyways."

"But there was work to be done, and me and Eddie decided we'd do the honors."

"Simón Cabrón. So we went out looking for that fucker," Eddie said and then cleared his throat. "I mean, that guy."

I cut in here. "Madrid, you wanna wait in the van?" But she shook her head at me, and so I left it at that.

"So we start looking, but we don't know what the hell we're looking for! You dudes were the only ones who really saw El Pinche. And it was freakin' dark out there, Man."

"Yeah, I know. I was out there lookin' for him, too. We were probably hearing each other movin' around, making everything worse because now his tracks are gonna be next to impossible to find with all of ours in the mix."

"Pshhh. No lie. We didn't think of that, Bro," Tom said.

I don't know why, but Tom was just pissing me off more and more each time he opened his mouth. I wasn't in the mood for him today. "So you didn't find him then, huh, Tommy?"

They both shook their heads in disgust.

"But here's the part that sucks," Tom said. "Now, Eddie's dad is looking for Javen."

"Why Javen?"

"Because, Dude. Things aren't adding up," Eddie said as he finished off his cigarette. He threw it on the ground and crushed it with his boot, puffing out the last lungful of smoke into the air. Eddie moved closer to me and started talking lower, like he'd gotten to the important part of the story. "Everybody had to talk to the police, and it started to look bad for Javen when they found out he was pissed at Joey and out on some rampage looking for him. Then somebody said he wanted to find Dolores, too, something about she owed him money. And then your story didn't jive with his story. And then there's that 9 mm Beretta..."

"What about it?"

"Dude, my dad ain't supposed to be saying shit to me, so you better keep this on the down low —"

"It wasn't traceable and Javen's was the only readable prints on the thing." Tommy was quick to finish for Eddie. It was weird, but Eddie never seemed to mind. Javen would kick my ass if I was always finishing his sentences.

"They're gonna be looking for your brown ass, too," Eddie said. "They got lots more questions."

Ed was getting tired of standing in his boots by this point, so he squatted down and pulled out another ciga-rette, this time from the pack wrapped in the sleeve of his t-shirt. He held it and kept talkin', not lighting it this time, like he knew it was too soon to be hitting another one.

"I already told them everything I could tell them," I said. I was feeling afraid all over again, like I wanted to throw up, Exorcist-style. "And so why didn't you guys tell them that Javen didn't do it?"

"Dude, they wanted to know if we saw Dolores or Joey get shot." Tommy said. "What were we supposed to do, lie? By the time we got there, Dolores was long gone and Joey was on his way. For all we knew it was Javen. That boy's got a temper."

Freakin' Tommy. I couldn't believe what I was hearing!

"Listen, Me and Madrid gotta go. I gotta find Javen."

I shook their hands and thanked them for the warning. When we got back into the van, Madrid pulled out her notebook.

What are you gonna do? she wrote.

What was I going to do? There was only one answer. "I'm gonna take you back to Ashlin's. And then I'm gonna go look for this guy. That's the only way Javen will be cleared, right? If I bring in the psycho?"

"I don't know," she said. "But I'm going with you."

"I don't think so, Madrid. We're talking about a rapist and a murderer."

"All the more reason for you not to be alone," she said as she brushed my arm with her soft hand. God, she was good at trying to convince me of something. But there was no way I could let her go. Ms. P. would kill me, for one. And it was dangerous.

"I can't," I whispered. It was hard getting those words out, especially since I wanted her company in a bad way.

And then she broke out with the notebook again. *Sonny, I'm going with you. And here's why: If you take me back to Ashlin's...I hate to say it, but I'm going to have to call your mom. You're right. It IS dangerous. And I'm not gonna let you go alone.*

"Period!" she yelled.

Oh, she was good. She was very, very good. It looked like I was going to get the privilege of her company. But this just meant the stakes were that much higher. I could not screw this up. "Okay, Madrid. You talked me into it."

She smiled. "And when we get through this and come back home, we can both be d-d-dead meat together."

And that's when I realized she really didn't need that notepad like she thought she did. Although I wasn't about to bring it to her attention.

"All right, Madrid. But before we go anywhere," I added. "We need to come up with a game plan."

Chapter 12
Antonia's Story

The house was warm and smelled like chocolate-chip cookies. It was dark outside, and my mommy wasn't home. But I wasn't afraid. I followed the smell that came from the kitchen, but I couldn't find the cookies, only more of the smell. Had I eaten them all? Maybe that's why my tummy hurt so much. I bent over, trying not to moan too loud. I didn't want to wake anybody. But it hurt so bad. I needed help. So I left the kitchen with the green cabinets and a round table and went into the living room. There was a cowboy movie on the big wooden TV. There was a Raggedy Ann doll on the flowered couch, but it wasn't mine. A big lamp was on the table next to the couch. What else was on that table? Something shiny. I stepped even closer. The shiny thing was a gun, like the one the man on TV was using.

I picked it up. It was heavy. I looked inside the little hole at the end, but I couldn't see anything. It was dark in there. I turned it around and tried to hold it the way the man on TV was. But it was too heavy, so I had to use both hands. And then I got a pain so bad it made me bend over to hold my tummy, too. There was a loud bang. It made a baby start to cry. I started to cry, too.

"Antonia!" someone yelled. It scared me and I dropped the gun down on the table. There was another loud bang. And a ringing sound in my ears. My tummy hurted so bad that I was shaking.

The lady who yelled my name ran to the other room. Then she started to scream. I covered my ears and rolled into a ball on the floor. I was scared. Was I in trouble? Why was she yelling?

I got up and walked into the room where she was screaming. There were two little beds. One was empty. In the other one, I saw a little girl. She was lying down on her side asleep. Blood was squirting out of the back of her head. I got another pain and fell to the ground holding my tummy. I started shaking again, but this time it was because I was afraid.

The lady scooped me up and ran outside with me. We ran and ran. We left the crying baby, the smell of chocolate-chip cookies, and the little girl in the bed with blood squirting from her head.

I didn't want to leave without her. I yelled, "Stacia!" and squirmed like jelly to get out of the lady's arms. I fought and fought and hit her. But she was too strong.

"Stacia! Stacia!"

"Antonia! Antonia!"

"Leave me alone!" I yelled.

"Mi'ja! Wake up!"

"Stacia!"

My mom shook me until I finally awoke, clenching my stomach, covered in sweat, she and Javen hovering over me. I jumped into her arms, stiff with fear.

"It was just a dream," she reassured me. "It was just a dream."

"Who's Stacia?" Javen asked.

I pulled away from my mom, grabbed the tissue he handed me and thought for a minute.

Mom answered before I could. "Nobody, Javen. It was just a bad dream."

"No, Mom. I felt...." I couldn't explain the pain. Why? What was that dream about?

"It was just a dream. Just a bad dream." She was just as upset as I was. I could tell. She wiped my tears and kissed my forehead and clenched her jaw like someone who had just been given a shot of iron in their backside.

"Man, you weren't kidding when you said you had bad dreams! You were yelling bloody murder," Javen said. "Were you dreaming about last night?"

"No. I wasn't. I don't know what I was dreaming. It was horrible. There was a little girl. She was... she was..."

"That's enough, Antonia. There's no need in upsetting yourself all over again. It was just a very bad dream. You witnessed your good friend getting shot last night! Of course you're going to have nightmares. Fear will manifest itself in any way it can. If we tried analyzing everything that takes place in our minds while we're sleeping, we'd go crazy. You need to just let it go, Baby."

My mom spoke with that same agitated tone of voice she got every time I brought up the subject of her past. She had quit comforting me and had started chipping away at the nail polish on her left thumb. It made me suspicious of her intentions, but I said nothing. I was glad she was here to take care of me. Besides, I had more important things to care about — my God, Joey was dead; Adolph was missing.

"You're right, Mom."

And with those three words, a weight was magically lifted off of her shoulders. She lost the edge in her tone and her nervousness, shuffling me into the shower and telling Javen to get some more sleep while she ran out to get us breakfast.

Before stepping into the bathroom, I turned around. "Mom?"

"Yes?"

"Thank you."

"For what, mi'ja?"

"For everything. Just...everything."

Her eyes welled up with tears. "Anything for my girls."

The warm shower felt good against my tired body. I liked my showers hot and hard. I liked to inhale the steam, imagining it permeating into my brain, clearing the clutter. The beads of hot water scattered across the stretch of my back and neck, relaxing my tense muscles. And yet it was doing nothing to erase the vividness of my dream. It wasn't as easy to forget as my mother would have liked.

I thought about that pain in my stomach, that horrible stomach ache. It was right where my scar was. I reached down and touched the small scar on the lower right side of my belly, trying to remember what it must have felt like. I had no recollection of how I got it. But I had never really tried to remember, either. I believed my mother when she said a little boy cut me with a piece of glass at the park when I was three. Why shouldn't I? Who would lie about something like that?

But the dream — it was so real I could smell it. And the pain in my stomach was so genuine I couldn't endure it. My mother never wanted me to look too deeply into anything. I, on the other hand, had to sift through all information, processing the most minute of details.

I repeated my mother's words again in my head. *Fear will manifest itself in any way it can.* But as a little girl? I couldn't understand why.

I shut my eyes and traced the line of my tiny scar, trying to conjure up a memory. Any memory. I pictured myself lying in a hospital bed, scared to death while a nice man sang "John Jacob Jingleheimer Smith." Over and over, he sang this to me. And then a young woman, a nurse walked in. She pulled back the sheet and gently cleaned my belly just before putting a needle into my arm. Once she was done, they wheeled me down a long hallway. All I could see were the lights up above while the nurse held one hand and a man with long hair held the other.

Was this a memory or just my overzealous imagination? I tried to force more details into focus, but there were none. Maybe my mother was right. Maybe I ought to just let it go. What I needed to focus on was remembering every minute detail about Adolph so that they could find that bastard.

After filing the report, we drove back to the hospital to pick up the Suvee. And much to our surprise, Ms.

Goretti's minivan pulled in right behind us. I'd never been so thankful for Javen to be right or so glad to see that minivan in all my life. I didn't even give Sonny a chance to park. As Mom slowed down to find a parking space, I jumped out of her car and ran to Sonny's window and told him to stop so I could give him a hug. That's when I noticed who he was with.

Madrid! *Was this the hippie's doing?* She smiled a sad sort of smile as I stopped running alongside the van and waited for them to park. I inhaled deeply and could still smell the scent of the forest on me, part of me wanting to sniff the invigorating woodsy smell 'til I could sniff it no more. Another part of me was antsy to get home and change my clothes and shoes, separate myself from everything crazy and unfamiliar about my life.

As I waited on Sonny to park, Mom came around and draped her arm around my shoulder and kissed my head. "How are you holding up?" she asked.

"I'm fine." It was a canned answer, something that didn't have a shred of thoughtfulness in it because I wasn't at all interested in talking with her at that moment. Sonny was here, and I was happy to see him. Madrid was here, and I desperately needed to talk to her.

"Why did Madrid and Sonny come back up to Silver City?" Mom asked next.

"I don't know," I answered without so much as considerate eye contact. "But now that there's nothing keeping us in this town, I'll just take her back with me in the Suvee."

"Antonia," Javen said with a scolding tone.

"What?"

"Can you hear yourself?"

"What?" I repeated, this time a little louder so that he understood I wasn't joking; I had no idea what his tone was about, much less the question. There was nothing keeping us in this town.

"You're acting so...." But he couldn't finish saying whatever was on his mind. He continued to stare at me like my face was covered with boils, or like I'd just gotten my nose pierced. It was disgust or utter shock, I wasn't sure which.

Meanwhile, Sonny looked like he was on a date, running around to the passenger side and opening Madrid's door for her. It was sweet, yet strange.

As they both walked over, I ran up to Sonny and threw my arms around him.

"You had us worried, you know," he said, taking the words right out of my mouth.

"We were the worried ones!" I said. "Are you okay?"

"Don't I look okay?"

I smiled and tweaked his nose. "Better than ever. I wish I could stay and chat, Sonny, but I've got to get back home." I walked over to Madrid, leaving Javen and Mom to finish welcoming Sonny back.

"Antonia, where are you going?" Mom asked.

"Home."

"Hey," Madrid said as I approached her.

"Hey," I answered back, reaching into my pocket for my keys. "You ready to go?"

"Huh?" Of course she didn't know what I meant. "Let's go home. You can ride with me in the Suvee."

"But..."

"We can talk about it on the drive home. Come on." I grabbed her hand and pulled her in the direction of the Suvee. "See you at home, Mom.

"Jav, Son, I'll call you guys later!" I yelled without waiting for a response.

Madrid got into the car and her expression said that she still wasn't over the confusion. As we drove away, she continued to look at Sonny like she was being kidnapped. I wanted her to forget about Joey, Sonny, and the hospital for a moment and just relax so we could talk.

As we got onto the highway, I found myself speeding from pure anxiety. I wondered how to get Madrid to open up so that we might have a decent conversation. If there was one thing I wished I could fix for her, it was the stutter. We didn't speak much and weren't close sisters in the least. But when she did try to speak to me, her stuttering added to the strain that was already there. I didn't understand it. Not the stuttering, but why there was strain in the first place. It was as though I felt guilty whenever we'd start getting close.

She was so much like our mother. Secretive. They were the mysterious ones. And so unapologetic for it. Neither of them noticed that I felt isolated or different. I don't think they really knew me at all, not like Joey, or even Javen and Sonny. My boys knew when I was mad without the sighs and frowns, the heaved shoulders, or the slamming of things. And vice versa. I couldn't really tell when Madrid was upset, much less happy. It was a sad thing. I loved my family, and I knew my family loved me. But we were like a school of fish, swimming together through the vast ocean by mere instinct, always looking straight ahead, barely aware of one another's presence.

Maybe we could be closer if it weren't for the lies, the secrets. The fire and Matthew's death — those were things that, until now, I couldn't bring myself to question. Maybe I just hadn't had the energy...or the desire.

But Mom always said she didn't have any living relatives, and that lie was something I had a hard time overlooking. She hid the fact that she had a sister. She and her little secrets. I never told her I knew otherwise. I figured she wasn't the only one who could keep a secret. I could hide things, too. Well, one thing, anyway. I never told her about the letter that had come in the mail three years ago, the letter I'd opened even though it was addressed to her. The one with no return address postmarked from San Diego. It was typed and didn't have a signature at the bottom, and it had been written to say her sister — a sister I'd never known she had — had committed suicide on New Year's Eve.

At first, I thought it was some sort of sick joke. But the more I read it and reread it, the more I believed its contents.

Dear Felicia,

I hope this letter finds you and the girls doing well. I can only imagine how beautiful they must be after all these years. How beautiful you all are. God, how I miss you.

I write only to tell you about your sister Alicia. She never did recover from the grief. I'm afraid depression claimed her life this New Year's Eve. Please don't feel guilty. Please keep strong. I'm only telling you this because she is your sister and I thought you would want to know.

Who would write such a letter? It didn't sound malicious or cruel. It sounded very normal. Anonymous, but normal.

I still had it tucked away, Mom none the wiser. After keeping it hidden for so long, I was almost afraid to give it to her now. Telling someone their sister committed suicide isn't exactly the easiest thing to say, especially if a person doesn't say it immediately. I justified my secrecy by telling myself she didn't want me to know of Alicia's existence, anyway. I didn't know any of her family, our family. I wondered why someone thought Mom would be feeling guilty over her sister's suicide; I wondered why she hadn't kept in touch with her, why she didn't already know about this news for herself. Maybe she did. Maybe she just didn't mention it, like so many other things she failed to mention.

I'd come full circle. Now I was back to wondering what Madrid knew about us, about our past.

"Why are you in s-s-s-such a hurry to get home?" she asked.

"I'm not in a hurry to get home, Madrid. I was just in a hurry to talk to you."

Already my words did something to frighten her because her face tightened and she appeared apprehensive.

"Don't worry. I just wanna talk. We never talk."

"Th-th-th-that's because of my, my...you know."

"No, it's not because of the stutter. I don't believe that. It's because of me. I haven't made the time to get to know you. And for that...for that I'm really sorry, Madrid."

She wasn't buying it, I could tell, if not from her face, then from her words. "S-s-s-so...what did you want to talk about?"

Nirvana was still playing on the CD player. I didn't remember it making its way back in there. In fact, I had no recollection at all of music playing on the drive back to the hospital the night before.

"Smells Like Teen Spirit," the same song we roared to at the top of our lungs only yesterday. I shuddered, quickly hitting eject.

"I want you to tell me what you know about Mom or our past or San Diego. I'll take anything you've got."

She wouldn't look at me while I spoke and when I was done, she still remained pensive. I gave her plenty of time to gather her thoughts in hopes that it would cut back on the stuttering, but not even a full two minutes seemed to be enough.

I felt like I'd been patient enough. "Fine then, Madrid. I don't know why I thought —"

"Pull over," she interrupted.

And so I did. I didn't wait for her to change her mind.

"I-I-I have too much to say, s-s-s-so I'm going to write," she said.

My heart fluttered with impatience as she started to write.

I'm sorry for not talking about this with you sooner. But I was still trying to figure it all out for myself first.

"Yeah, don't worry about that. What's important is that you're telling me now, right?" I said, poorly hiding my impatience.

Yes, but there's still A LOT that I don't know. I've been trying to find stuff out through the Internet. Mom had a brother, did you know?

"No, I didn't," I answered. What I was hoping she knew had more to do with me and maybe a little girl or our father, our aunt who'd committed suicide, the house that burned down. Mom's brother, while significant, was on the low end of my priority list.

Yeah, and according to his website, he's been looking for her all these years. He's posted pictures of his two girls (who look eerily like me) and only talks about the present, not at all about their past. But I'm getting way ahead of myself....

"Yeah, just start from the beginning, Madrid. If that's even possible." I tried to remain calm, even though I wanted to bypass the notepad and just stick a straw into the back of her head to extract everything I needed to know.

Okay. Do you remember the trip to Oklahoma?

I nodded. I could've been sarcastic, but it wasn't the time. There was no time, as far as I was concerned.

That's when I started to learn everything that I know. When we first got there, I asked Jewel if I could use her bathroom. She said the toilet in the hall was acting up and told me to use the one in her bedroom. Do you remember that?

"No, not really."

Madrid rolled her eyes then kept writing.

Anyway, I really didn't have to use the bathroom. I just wanted an excuse to look around, to figure out who this person was and why we were there. It was a weird trip, wouldn't you agree?

She lifted up the notebook so I could read before continuing. "Yes, it was all very weird. But don't worry about lifting up; I can read as you write."

Well, anyway, in her room there was a picture of mom and a man. I KNEW there was more to her relationship with Jewel Wisdom.

"Who was the man?"

I took the picture out of its frame and turned it over. It said Felicia and Matthew.

"Madrid, we know that Dad's name was Matthew."
She wrote faster, harder and, subsequently, sloppier.
Yeah, but did you know his last name is...
I couldn't read what the last name said, but it was definitely not Pacheco. "I can't read that last word."
"Wisdom!" she shouted.
"What?"
"The picture s-s-s-said Felicia Pacheco and Matthew Wisdom."
I was confused. "So he was related to Jewel?"
She's our grandmother. That's her son.
"What? Why didn't they say something? Did you ask Mom about it?"
No, but the next day when you and Mom went into town to the grocery store and I stayed behind, I asked Jewel some questions.
"And...."
And I didn't want to be obvious because I figured she didn't want us to know she was our grandmother or she would have just said so. So I started an innocent conversation by asking for some tea bags.
"Wow, I can't believe how sneaky you are. I wouldn't have thought to be sneaky about it."
"I know," she said.
She ended up inviting me to have some of her tea because she said there wasn't enough sun left in the day for me to make it proper. Meanwhile, I just tried to ask questions that anyone might ask.
"Like what?" I was at the edge of my seat hanging on every last word she wrote.
I asked if she had a husband. She said she did once, but she left him in San Diego and came back home because that city just wasn't big enough for the both of them.
"So she lived in San Diego. Did she talk about Matthew?"
She nodded. *She said her son used to stutter, too, so she wanted me to relax and know that she wouldn't rush me*

when I spoke. (She was having a hard time with my writing, too.)

"It's fine when you slow down," I said. "But don't slow down now! What else did she say about Matthew? Did she actually admit that his name was Matthew?"

"*You* need to slow down."

I smiled at her. This was so cool. It was the most talking we'd ever done, even if there wasn't much "talking" going on. "I'm sorry. Finish."

Anyway, she told me her son lived in San Diego. She said, "He's been teaching at the university there for years and years."

"She talked about him in the present tense? As if he's not dead?"

Again, she nodded.

She said he was born and raised in San Diego, so that's home to him. (She said you have to be a special person to live "out in these parts.") Then she said she used to see MATTHEW twice a year. I'm not sure, but I think she let that slip by accident. She said traveling was getting hard on her old bones and he was very busy and very depressed. Anymore, she said it's once a year or every other year that she sees him. She said....

Madrid stopped and gave her tired fingers a shake and wiggle. She tried talking again. "I-I-I asked if she had any grandk-k-k-kids."

"And?"

"She said no."

"NO?" I wouldn't have pegged Jewel as a liar. She seemed more like a hem and hawer. I suppose anyone can become a liar if the stakes are high enough. But what could possibly be the payoff for lying to your grandkids about having grandkids?

"There's one more thing..." Madrid said.

"What?"

"I found another picture.. in m-m-m-mom's room. It was you and..."

There's never many radio stations to choose from driving down this road; most of the good stations make their way here from El Paso or Las Cruces and only if the wind is just right and we're facing due east on a cloudless day, or something like that. So after I ejected Nirvana, it defaulted to Santa Ana's only local station that comes in loud and clear: country/western music from KOZS.

It didn't seem so loud when it was Merle Haggard and George Strait. But suddenly it turned to the local news.

This just in: José Diaz, the Santa Ana High senior who was shot last night near the San Francisco Springs, died at Alliance Hospital in Silver City early this morning. Witnesses say Diaz was shot by the same man who allegedly raped and murdered Santa Ana High senior and cheerleader Dolores Teran last night during a camping trip known as Senior Ditch Day. The suspect is described as Caucasian, in his mid-twenties with short, blond hair, approximately five-foot-ten inches tall and may appear to be injured. Grant County Deputy Sheriff Manny Fuentes stated that anyone with information should contact the Sheriff's Office immediately. Principal Kent Garrett was unavailable for comment to announce whether the graduation ceremony will still take place today or be rescheduled due to the deaths of the two students. Diaz would have been senior class valedictorian. We here at KOZS would like to extend our condolences to both families and say that you are in our thoughts and prayers. We'll be back right after these messages.

Joey's death was hitting me in waves. Joey is dead. Joey is *dead*. *Joey* was dead. I looked into the back seat and saw the proof in my blood-stained upholstery.

My mind suddenly felt as though it had been thrown into a deep freezer. It was shutting down. And yet the rest of my body went into overdrive — racing, spinning, convulsing.

"Antonia!"

I looked over at Madrid who was crying and cringing with fear, like she was standing witness to an exorcism. When she tried speaking, her voice came out muffled, as though someone had their hand over her mouth. Like Dolores. It was her sitting there. Dolores. Bruised and bloody. Naked. Trying to make herself heard through my screams and the muffling hand over her mouth.

The next thing I knew, Javen and Sonny were parked behind us. Javen jumped out of Sonny's passenger door and opened my driver's side door. He caught me as I stepped out blinded with tears.

Before I knew it, Javen was pulling the Suvee into my driveway. My head was on his shoulder and he was gently combing my hair back with his hand. I sat up and looked at him.

He got out and went to my side. He opened the car door for me and helped me inside. He took me to my room and told me to lie down while he went to the kitchen and got me a glass of ice water. He asked me to sit up so I could take a sip.

"Can I get you anything? An aspirin or something?"

I shook my head.

"I'll stay until your mom gets back." And just as he said that, she pulled in.

We both looked toward the window and then back at one another. We were like two tumbleweeds clinging to a fence. I knew he didn't want to leave me any more than I wanted him to leave. And so I grabbed his wrist and held on tight to keep him from blowing away.

He got up and went to my door, closed it and locked it. He turned on the stereo to drown all sound and went back to my bed and lay next to me. I rested my head on his chest, and we held each other close, guiltlessly, as I slowly drifted to sleep.

Chapter 13
Javen's Story

Icould've slept for three days straight, but Antonia's nightmare wasn't anywhere near finished; I woke up from all her moaning and squirming.

I'd heard somewhere before that you aren't supposed to wake a person when they're having a bad dream, but Ms. Pacheco didn't seem to have a problem with it earlier at the hotel. And since Antonia has bad dreams all the time, she must've known what she was doing when she woke her. So I figured it was okay to shake her arm, touch her cheek, hoping she might just roll over and calm down. Nothing. I should've known it wouldn't be that easy.

"Antonia," I said softly. Still nothing.

"Antonia," I said a little louder. Her crying just seemed to get worse.

I couldn't yell any louder. Well, I could've, but I didn't want to. I decided to leave it to the expert.

Ms. Pacheco was hanging up the phone when I walked into the kitchen.

"Well, graduation is officially cancelled," she said. "That was your principal. If all goes well, it'll be in two weeks...not so close to the funeral services."

"Good," I said. "Ms. Pacheco, Antonia is crying pretty hard in her sleep. She's not screaming like she was earlier, so I didn't know what the right thing to do was, whether to wake her or —"

Before I could finish my sentence, she was down the hall and on her way to Antonia's bedroom. Meanwhile, someone was knocking on their door.

"Javen, will you get that, mi'jo?" she said before disappearing into Antonia's room.

When I opened the door, Ed's dad, Manny Fuentes, was standing there. He was nothing like his lean, long-haired, dope-smoking son. They didn't come much more clean-cut than Manny. He was just your typical pot-bellied retired military/law enforcement known throughout the county for his Gestapo tactics. He was a cliché with his neat, black mustache and crew-cut hair. I imagine the only thing he might've had in common with Ed was a tattoo hiding somewhere on his back or upper arm, but I couldn't say for sure.

"Javen. Just the man I'm looking for."

"Hey, Mr. Fuentes."

"Son, I need you to come with me."

I didn't want to leave Antonia. "Why?" I asked.

"We need to ask you a few more questions about last night."

Last night. Last night had been a long chain of re-enactments. *I was standing here. Joey and Antonia were over there. Dolores was lying right here. The killer was where you are. I did this. He did that. Yes, I handled the gun.*

There were a few things I'd left out. I didn't want to make it seem like Sonny was a stupid-ass, so I lied about how the killer got away from right underneath him. I lied about why I was looking for Joey, too. I didn't say I was out to kick his ass. I knew that would raise eyebrows. And so I said Sonny and I got worried when they'd wandered off for so long. I said that we considered it our friendly responsibility to search 'em out. *That's when I heard the first gunshot. We followed it, then we heard the second. We snuck up on them, but the shootings had already happened. No, we didn't actually see who did the shootings. But we know it was him. This blond guy was holding the gun. We managed to wrestle it away from him. Yes, my prints will be all over that gun. But you should find others, as well. Sonny's. The killer's. Yes, Sonny held it first. Then I took over because Joey needed help. I dropped the gun and the killer got away.*

"Why didn't you just help Antonia with Joey? Why did Sonny have to hand over the gun?"

"Because he's bigger and stronger. Sonny could pick Joey up and run with him a lot better than I could. It seemed like the right thing to do at the time (another lie). I realize now that it was a mistake."

"Why didn't you try to bring Dolores to the hospital as well?"

"Because it was obvious that she was dead! Joey was still alive! We had to get him help quick; we couldn't waste any time at all!"

I could hear the questions pounding in my head all over again while Antonia moaned and groaned in the background.

"Does this have to be right now?" I asked Mr. Fuentes.

"Yes."

There was this empty pause because I expected him to say more, to explain to me why it had to be right now. I got nothing.

What the hell was left to ask, anyway? I'd already told them everything I knew. Had somebody given a different story? Is that what this was about? Were they just desperate to arrest somebody?

"All right. Can you wait a second so I can tell Ms. Pacheco that I'm leaving?"

He nodded.

When I walked back into Antonia's bedroom, Ms. P was trying to coax her awake in the same way that I had been, softly, gently, except she was doing it in Spanish.

"Mi'ja, despierta. Por favor, Antonia, despierta."

"Ms. Pacheco, I have to leave."

She was completely distracted, not even looking up at me as she said okay.

"All right...well, I guess I'll see you later. Best of luck waking her."

Maybe it was the hint of sarcasm in my voice that made her look up. "What? Where are you going, Javen? Is Sonny here?"

Was it wrong of me to be happy that she took her attention off of Antonia for a minute to notice that I was leaving? Was it wrong that I wanted someone to care that the sheriff was here to pick me up?

"No, it's not Sonny. The sheriff is here and says I need to go back with him because —"

"Manny Fuentes?"

"Yeah."

As she got up to walk to the door, she immediately got an outta-my-way look on her face.

"Hello, Mr. Fuentes. How can I help you?"

"You can't, Felicia. But Javen can. He needs to come with me."

"Why?" she asked almost before the last word was out of his mouth.

"With all due respect, you aren't his legal guardian so —"

"Manny, I think you and I both know that he is already eighteen. Nobody is his legal guardian.

"But, as you know, this is my house. He's staying with me. And he doesn't have legal representation at the moment. So what is it that you want right now?"

Mr. Fuentes couldn't hide his irritation, clenching his jaw in a way that said he would give anything to put Ms. P in her place.

He scoffed and grinned. "Nobody needs legal representation, Felicia."

"Good, then I'll give him a ride to your office shortly. Now if you'll excuse me; I need to be with my daughter. She and Javen just lost their best friend last night.

"We'll see you a little later, Mr. Fuentes."

Manny Fuentes exhaled audibly and put his hand on the closing door. "All right, Felicia. Have it your way. I'll give you an hour to get him to the station. If he doesn't show, I'll have a warrant for his arrest next time I knock."

Chapter 14
Sonny's Story

So we meet again," I said to her as she got in through the passenger side door. I didn't open it for her this time, but only because I wasn't expecting her to be coming with me.

"I-I-I can't sit in her back seat. It's...it's...."

This was bad. I put my hand on her shoulder. "It's okay, Madrid. I'm sorry to interrupt, but you don't have to say it. I wouldn't want to sit back there, either." I put the key back into the ignition and started her up. "I'll take you home."

Our game plan had consisted of writing a note for both our parents, which we did, and then stopping in Silver City, hopefully catchin' the Suvee alone so I could get a change of clothes, money, and food from my bag before headin' back for the forest.

We thought luck was on our side when we pulled into the parking lot at the hospital and saw the Suvee. That was seconds before we saw the whole group of 'em standing out there, like they'd been expecting us or somethin'.

"But w-w-w-what about the plan?" Madrid asked as we headed back south.

It was a good question.

"I don't know," I answered, feelin' like one of the jokes that dribbles out of Dad's mouth and lands flat on the cold floor. I was an embarrassment. I let bad guys get away, and I didn't have the gumption to make it right once and for all.

"I'm thinkin' it wasn't meant to be, Madrid. It's too crazy right now. You should be home with your family. Anyway, I didn't even get the chance to fish out some cash from my bag.

"And what's up with my mom not sending the cops out to look for me yet?" I asked out loud, without realizing I was asking it out loud.

Madrid was only half listening. She shrugged, her eyes fixed on something ahead of us.

I was preoccupied, too. On thoughts of the Gila. Imagining our campsite roped off like it always is in the movies. It was federal land, so I could already picture the crime scene crawling with forest rangers and men wearing those caps and jackets with the letters FBI embroidered on them. I could see them scratching their heads because there were about a hundred different footprints and one particularly large set that went in circles. There's no way I could have taken a fifteen-year-old girl to a sight like that...

"Sonny, I—"

"Can I interrupt you just one more time?"

She didn't like that, I could tell by the look on her face.

"I swear, I'll never do it again. I just want you to know that I appreciate you offering to come with me today. I mean, not many people would be willing to do that! It's huge. And so I just wanted to say thanks now while I'm thinkin' of it, before I let it get buried in all this...."

Madrid smiled, and that said plenty. She didn't even have to speak. I could tell I was forgiven for interrupting, maybe even for considering taking her out there in the first place.

Unfortunately, I made her lose her train of thought. Maybe that was a good thing. "You were w-w-willing to search for the killer, too."

I chuckled. "Yeah, well, I've come to my senses since. I don't know what I was thinkin'. Where would I have started looking for that dude? I'm sure he's halfway to Georgia by now. And say we got lucky and actually found him... then what?"

"I'm already t-t-t-tired of thinking about it," she said.

"Amen," I yelled. "So how 'bout we change the subject?"

"Yes!" she said. "But...c-c-can you read and drive?"

"No, I'm sorry, not unless you want to end up in the bar ditch. But let me take this opportunity to say that this is me you're talking to. Santino. And with Santino, there aren't any rules to follow. There aren't any time limits to maintain or subjects too dicey to bring up. You just take your sweet time and say what you please with me."

She looked as though she was about to cry. *Shit.* I was shootin' for amusing. Another failed mission. "I'm sorry," I whispered.

"No," she said. "Thank you, Santino." She came across and kissed me on the cheek.

Impulse told me to pull over, press my luck, take that cheek kiss to the next level. She was so beautiful and smelled so nice. But the gentleman in me decided it was best to keep drivin'. Maybe it wasn't the gentleman, so much as it was the chicken-shit afraid she'd scream and want out of the van.

"So, how'd you get th-th-that name, anyway?" she asked, putting a big red stop sign in front of my yearning.

"Well, since you asked so nicely, I'll tell you. I'm named after my grandpa who was named after Saint Anthony — you know, San Antonio? Santino, San Antonio, get it? It's an Italian thing. See, I'm from a long line of adopters. My Italian grandparents, Santino and Sofia, started it all. That's where I get the Goretti. They couldn't have kids, so they adopted Dad, who is a Navajo. Mom and Dad adopted me, just for the hell of it I guess. I'm obviously African-American. My mom is just as Chicana as you are.

"So I like to tell people I get to mark all the little boxes on forms except the Asian one, and even that's not a guarantee. As far as I'm concerned, I'm Black, White, Hispanic and Native American."

She was looking at me like she didn't know what to say next. I usually got questions like, "So how did your Italian family end up with a Navajo kid? And how did a Navajo kid end up with a Black one? And how did the lot of you end up here in Santa Ana, New Mexico?" But maybe when you have to write everything down in a notepad, a lot of the crap gets cut out.

She crossed her legs and started chewing on her middle fingernail. I guessed she was feeling nervous again. So I tried to ease her tension. "So that's me in a nutshell! Or maybe a clamshell since —"

"I didn't know that," she said, this time interrupting me. "Sorry to interrupt."

"No, it's cool," I said, nudging her to let her know I got it. "Which part didn't you know?"

She laughed and quit biting her nail. "Well, all of it, of course. But I was referring to you being adopted. And n-n-named after St. Anthony."

"Pretty weird, huh?" I couldn't help noticing that her stuttering was tapering off a little.

She smiled again, wider this time. "Antonia's named after him, too."

I already knew that, but I acted surprised anyway.

"So how'd *you* get your name?"

She got quiet. "I don't know," she finally said. "Big f-f-family secret."

"Y'all got more than your fair share of those, don't you?"

"Yeah...but I think we all know m-m-more than we admit to knowing."

"So why the secrecy?"

"I stutter. I don't know what th-th-their excuse is."

We were about ten miles down the road from the Pacheco's ranchette, and I was still thinkin' about the killer in the back of my mind, still praying for some sort of a miracle while I stared into the highway with its roadkill, mile markers and hitchhikers. *Hitchhikers.* Or should I say, *a hitchhiker. Could it be?*

"Did you just see that guy?" I asked Madrid.

"What guy?"

That answered that.

"Madrid, do you believe in ghosts?"

"I don't know. Why do you ask?"

"Remind me someday to tell you about my Mima's ghost," I said, slowing down and pulling over.

"Why not now?" she asked.

"Because right now we're gonna turn around and pick one up."

I pulled up ahead of him, just like the last time. He was grinning, but this time real distrustfully.

"Don't worry," I said as I stepped out of the van and opened the back door for him. "I ain't got beer to throw in your face...not that I'd do that anyway."

"Is this an offer for a ride?" he asked.

A *foreigner*. I don't know why, but I'd'a never guessed it. "Yes. Yes, it is, sir."

He stepped into the backseat and I swung the door shut for him.

"Sorry about the mess back there."

He didn't respond.

"So where to?" I asked.

"You tell me, Santino."

Already, that made two people in one day who called me by my real name, a name that neither of 'em were supposed to know. Not that it was a big secret. But it wasn't like Mike or Bob, either, a name you could guess at and get lucky.

Madrid was lost, and that was enough to get her nervous again. "Who-Who-Who..."

I'd been hopeful that the stutter was sort of fading out. And just as I thought that, Mr. Hitchhiker reached over and touched her shoulder.

"I'm just a thirsty stranger," he said. "No more, no less."

If I didn't know better, I'd'a said she exhaled that stutter like a slither of smoke just as he spoke to her. It would be the last time I ever heard that girl stammer.

"Sonny, do you have anything in here to drink?" she asked, completely forgetting that she was a little bit scared of him no more than a second before.

But the answer to her question was no. Not water, not tea, not even half a can of hot pop stuffed under a seat cushion somewhere.

"Sorry, I don't."

"That's okay. We can get something at my place. Sir, can you wait just a while longer?"

"You never say where you need to go," the hitchhiker said to me instead of answering her question.

"Where I need to go? Well, where I need to go is home. But where I want to go is where I was yesterday."

"Why?"

"Because I need to find someone."

"Then, where you need to go is where this someone is located. Yes?"

"Yeah, but I don't know where that is exactly."

"Let's keep going," he said. "Home."

I laughed. "You want to go to *my* home?"

"Parlate italiano?" he asked.

"Poco."

He winked at Madrid. "I am sorry. This is rude."

"No, it's fine. Really.

"Actually, I didn't know you spoke Italian, Sonny."

"Well, like I told him, just a little."

A few short miles of blacktop, and the hitchhiker asked me to turn right. Right back to the Pacheco's place. I was confused. But we didn't make it all the way back to their driveway. "You can drop me here," he said, pointing to the side of the road.

"Here?" I repeated.

"Yes, here."

I pulled over and parked, opening the door for him again.

He handed me the backpack that he had been carrying around with him.

"What's this for?" I asked. Thank you might have been more appropriate, but my words were already halfway out before I second-guessed myself.

"For later," he answered.

"Prendete la buona cura di questa donna giovane. Ha bisogno di buon amico," he said to me after hugging Madrid goodbye and just before walkin' away.

"Lo faro. Grazie por tutto." I would definitely take good care of this fine, young lady.

"Where's he going?" Madrid asked me.

I didn't know. And asking him was out of the question as he'd already disappeared into nothingness. We were left no wiser than before we'd picked him up.

The sky was getting cloudy. I could even hear the rumbling of thunder off in the distance, kinda like my stomach.

"So what's in the bag?" she asked next.

"Boy, you're just full of questions, aren't you?"

She grinned as she pulled it out of my hands and started to unzip it. Her face looked confused as she peered inside. She pulled out a long piece of rope and a red t-shirt. "You know what these are for?" She asked as she put the rope and t-shirt back into the bag and zipped it back up.

"Not a clue."

The clouds were stickin' around, getting thicker and darker, actually. I could see goosebumps all over Madrid's arms.

"You're cold," I said.

"Just a little." I pulled her closer to my warm body and hugged her in toward my chest. I could feel her nervous heartbeat and hear it pounding over the sound of the wind and her shivering breath.

"Still?" I asked.

"Yeah, still."

"I don't think I can bring you much closer," I said.

But she got closer still. Closer still, until my breath was mixed with hers like the different shades of browns in our hands. She wasn't shivering anymore; she was melting into me, and me into her. I could have held her forever. But the thunder sounded pretty close. I knew that I had to get her indoors.

As we got to the door, we heard the sound of Antonia yelling. I didn't wait for an invitation. I just followed Madrid inside.

Chapter 15
Antonia's Story

The passengers on a white, wooden roller coaster filled the air with screams every few seconds. There was a pizza place across the street from the beach, and the people sitting outside ate from slices too big for their plates. A colorful group of people gathered under a tree; one guy played a guitar while the others sang along. A mother and her young son rollerbladed past me on the sidewalk that ran parallel to the ocean. There was a cool mist from the sea. It gave me chills. I buried my feet in the wet sand and wrapped my arms around myself, feeling a breath of wind in my hair.

Another group of people began walking toward me. Four. As they came closer, I made out three familiar faces. Joey's, the hippie's, and my own. The other woman was a taller, thinner version of my mother. She smiled and revealed a gap between her two front teeth. I knew that smile. I knew that gap. It frightened me. I looked back at Joey, who was also smiling at me. He was wearing his cowboy hat, his faded Wranglers, his dusty white t-shirt. He smiled and waved at me. My chills instantly disappeared. I wanted to scream with joy and relief, knowing he was alive and well. I waved back and stood, feeling the most urgent need to run to him, to hold him and feel his solidness, his safe embrace. But then I remembered there was that third person. Me. She, too, was smiling. She had hair cropped short just like mine. She wore a v-neck tank top that matched the one I was wearing, crimson. Her cutoff Levi's were exactly like the ones I was wearing too. She was barefoot, just like me. I would have believed it was me, but between her breasts was a reddish mark. I knew that mark. I looked at her face again, her golden hair and skin reflecting the warmth of the sun, her gray eyes. But that mark on her chest, her strawberry...her"strawberry patch."

"Stacia?"

She smiled knowingly and held open her arms.

I tripped through the sand, over people and towels, beach bags and ice chests. I couldn't get to her fast enough. When I was finally two feet in front of her, so close that I could see the specks of blue in her gray eyes, I reached out to touch her face, to make sure she was real. She was. She wrapped her arms around me, and I held on tight for fear that she might disintegrate like my memories. I could actually feel her warm breath in my hair, smell the baby shampoo.

"My Stacia."

I pulled back and examined her face again, running my fingers over the contours of her eyes, her jaw, her lips. I giggled with excitement. It was like Christmas. She was as real as I was. How could I have ever forgotten? She held my hands with hers, occasionally letting go to wipe my tears.

"Please don't cry," she said as she sat down and pulled me down beside her. "You're making me cry."

I laughed. "I've never cried so much in my entire life as I have in the last twenty-four hours."

She hugged me all over again.

"Why did you leave me?"

She mulled over the question for awhile. "It's complicated," she finally said.

"Then answer this if you can. How could I have forgotten you?"

"You were just a baby. We were babies."

"I know, but —"

"If I was truly forgotten, you wouldn't have remembered me now." Stacia was soaking me in as much as I was her.

There were so many questions. I didn't know where to begin. "Where have you been all this time?"

"With you," she said.

I didn't understand the answer. I think she could tell. "I was always visiting you," she said.

"When? Where was I?"

She squeezed my hand. "It's hard to explain, but...you were there, too! Like in your dreams. All I ever wanted was for you to remember me. I'm sorry for the pain I've caused you, Antonia."

"Why didn't you just show yourself like you are now?"

"I couldn't show you my face. You wouldn't have understood. You would have only seen yourself. The time wasn't right, anyway...not until now, when you can be sure it's me, with all these people here you know and love."

I looked up at the hippie. He winked in recognition of Stacia's words.

Joey came over to us. He bent over and kissed me, wiping my tears.

"And you!" I said.

"What?" he asked, looking exactly the same as he always did.

"What happened? You were supposed to be getting better."

He lifted his cowboy hat and scratched his head, as though he didn't know how to explain.

"You can't be gone, Joey."

He handed me a handkerchief from his back pocket and said nothing.

"Say something," I said. "Say it isn't true. I thought we had a deal, José Diaz."

"I did promise you something, didn't I?" he said.

"Yeah, so what happened?"

Again, he said nothing.

I turned away. He came closer, lifted my chin with his forefinger and gently coaxed my eyes back to his.

"How far back does your memory go, Antonia?"

I didn't feel like thinking about something so irrelevant and impossible to answer. I shrugged my shoulders in protest to the question.

"Antonia, think. Do you remember preschool? When you and I became friends?"

"Yes," I whispered.

"And do you remember how our mothers became friends as well?"

"Yes," I said slightly louder.

"In fact, our friendship may not have grown and held as fast as it did if it weren't for the friendship between our mothers.

"When you all first came to Santa Ana, your mom was very depressed. She had no one...she needed help in making the simplest of decisions, like which hairdresser to use, or where to find good produce. But more than that, she needed to talk and cry and 'confess.'

"My mom was more than happy to listen. And because of that, we got to know each other better and better all the time.

"Meanwhile, my mom slowly became aware of a lot of stuff from your past. One day your mom came to my mom with a manila envelope and said, 'If I die before seeing my daughters into adulthood, I want you to do something for me.' She asked that my mom hold onto this envelope and safe-keep it. Inside was a sort of journal of some of her memories, things she wanted you to know, but not until you were ready.

"Like she promised, my mother kept this envelope as safe from harm as she did her recipe for molé. But just last month your mom came and asked for it back. You see, she lived to see you become an adult after all.

"I know now that she never did share the contents of that envelope with you. And now that you're ready for your own truth, maybe she's ready too. She wants to share it with you. She prays for a miracle, a catalyst, every single day."

He hugged me hard and long and pressed his lips to my forehead. "Before I go, I need you to do me one last favor..."

"Anything."

"Anything?"

I nodded my head before knowing what I was agreeing to. And maybe it was because I believed that his favor would involve staying right there with him forever. Whatever was going through my mind, it definitely wasn't this: "Move on, Baby. Please don't waste any more time. Not another minute."

If he was here with Stacia, then it was true. I wasn't going to see him again.

"This can't be goodbye, Joe...."

He couldn't, or wouldn't, say it. If the silence wasn't speaking volumes, the guilty look on his face said it all.

"Say you'll at least be a part of my dreams," I pleaded. I turned to the hippie. "Please..." I begged.

"You have to stop looking back now," Joey said for him. "I soaked up all your time when I was alive. You can't waste anymore of it on me because there are so many people who need you right now; your mom..."

"You mean that woman who's been lying to me all my life?"

I clenched my heart and cried tired tears. "I lost my twin sister; I don't think my heart can bear losing you too, Joey. I'd rather die than —"

"Stop that! Antonia, don't you see?" He put my hand back on his own heart that still beat as strongly as mine. "You aren't three years old anymore. Nothing could make us disappear again."

The unfamiliar woman who had been standing there silently came closer to us.

Joey nodded in her direction. "Do you remember her, Antonia?"

The woman stood, looming, smiling her gap-toothed smile nervously at me as though to stimulate a memory. Her long hair was thin and graying. She came closer.

Closer still. I felt chained to the sand, unable to stand, run, even scream.

She quit smiling and quit coming closer when she saw how afraid I was.

"Antonia," Stacia said softly.

I quit staring at the woman and looked back at Stacia.

"You don't have to be afraid anymore."

But I was. I was terrified.

"Who are you?" I asked the woman.

Her mouth began to move, as though she were saying, "I...I...I..." but she didn't have a voice.

I stared at her through her struggle to speak until I realized where my fear was coming from.

"*You*! It was you, wasn't it? You killed my sister, didn't you? You're the one who took her away! *You killed Stacia!*"

I tried to stand, but I was being pulled down, almost magnetically. I couldn't breathe. I couldn't think straight.

And then the hippie said, "It's time to go."

With that, they all walked back in the direction from which they'd come. They didn't look back at me even once.

"Come back! Don't leave me here!"

But they did. They left me again. I wanted to die, to chase after my sister, my best friend, even the hippie. But I was paralyzed. I was confined to the sandy beach near the roller coaster.

I didn't want to go back. I was angry and hurt with my mother in ways that felt irreparable.

I awoke and squinted from the light. When I realized I was back, I sat bolt-upright in my bed; Mom, Madrid, Sonny and Javen were all staring at me. Mom reached to hold me, but I pushed her away.

I could tell from her face that she knew that I knew.

As soon as Sonny and Javen realized that I was awake, they excused themselves.

My mother left the room, too. When she came back, there was a manila envelope in her hand.

Chapter 16
Javen's Story

Before leaving the Pacheco's, I opened the back of Antonia's Suvee and grabbed my bag of essentials. I'd gone long enough without a toothbrush and deodorant. I couldn't stand my own self. The old me would have snatched up a beer for the road before shutting the hatch, but I passed it up without so much as a second thought. Instead, I thought about whether or not to take Joey's bag. What was in there that might be of interest? Books? Notepads? His money? Not! On all counts. What kind of an ass would take his dead friend's money? I decided there was only one reason to even touch it — to return it to his family when I would go give them my condolences. Then they could decide what to do with it.

As I yanked on the bag to unwedge it from between the cooler and the sleeping bags, a notebook fell out of the side pocket, opened to a page full of writing. I don't know how, but my eyes went straight to my name amid all the other words that were scribbled around it. I had to do some more debating, this time about whether I should make this thing my business and read it. Curiosity got the best of me right about the time Sonny revved his engine a little to let me know he was waiting. I decided I'd read it later in the privacy of Sonny's hall bathroom. I put the notebook back in the bag, passed on the beer, and slammed the back of the Suvee shut. I was anxious to get to his house, use the bathroom, read the parts of Joey's notebook that were about me, and see how Sonny's sisters' report cards ended up looking. I wanted to think about anything except what was going on in Antonia's room with her mom and sister.

"Glad you made it back, Sonnyboy."

Sonny laughed at that as he pulled out of their driveway. "You ain't got to lie for me, Bro."

"Sonny, I might be a lot of things, but a liar isn't one of them."

"Not according to Eddie."

"What the hell does that mean?"

"According to Eddie, our stories don't jive."

He could've just stopped there. I already knew the rest. "And I know you well enough to know that you tried covering for me last night, too. Didn't you?"

I sighed. "So you obviously didn't find that fucker Adolph."

"He has a name? How'd *you* learn it?"

"The road Sonny. Watch where you're going or pull over and let me drive." For as long as I'd known him, Sonny had never been too keen on multitasking. We were bouncing around like hail in a rainstorm as we rolled over four-foot-high mesquite bushes. No big deal if we were in a pickup and the goal was to have fun, but we were in his mom's van.

But he was only half-listening to me. "No, I didn't find our man Adolph."

I reached over and tugged at the wheel. This time I was the one half-listening.

"So what are we gonna do? Eddie says they're lookin' for *both* our asses."

"Well, I know for a fact that they're looking for me. I've already run into The Man Fuentes. I was able to sic Ms. Pacheco on him...stall him just a little while longer."

"But he'll be back. And when he catches up with you without Ms. P at your side, he's bound to be twice as pissed."

It was worse than that. He was bound to throw me in a pen and leave me there. He'd do the same to Sonny, just for being in my company. I suddenly remembered the face in the slats at the hotel and felt a jolt of electricity jump-start my two-sizes-too-small heart. None of this would be an issue if I'd only followed my gut and jumped that fence.

Now that Sonny had come back from the Gila empty-handed, there wasn't a doubt in my mind — Antonia wasn't just another girl, someone who managed to narrowly escape this guy. No, she was marked. Like the rest of us, Adolph had done made up his mind that she was something special. And he'd be back for her.

Sonny pulled over, almost as if he'd been reading my thoughts.

"I know what my problem is. What's yours?" I asked.

Sonny just sat there, his brain working on overtime. "I think we need to go back to the Pachecos'," he finally said. "I have a really bad feeling."

"Do you know something that I don't?"

"Yeah, I think I do."

And then he told me about the hitchhiker dude coming back for a visit. And the backpack.

"I can't believe I'm just now getting it! He was trying to tell me that what's-his-face is gonna show up there! God, I'm such a dumbass!"

"Adolph?"

"Adolph, Alex, Adam, whatever the hell his name is! He's coming back, I know it!"

I'd never seen Sonny so freaked out. But before I could tell him that I agreed, he was turning the van around and heading back.

"Don't be in such a big hurry, man. Pull over," I said while turning back to make sure there weren't any cars behind us since he hadn't bothered to look.

"Pull over?"

"Yeah, *pull over!*"

He turned and looked at me in a way I didn't recognize. Meanwhile, he kept driving. I suppose he didn't have to speak. His eyes and speed said it all: *Fuck you, Javen. You're not the boss of me.*

"You know, you've picked a fine time to grow a backbone, Sonny."

He laughed. "And you picked a fine time to take a piss!"

"I don't need to take a piss." I sighed and repeated myself, louder this time. "What I need is for you to *pull over!*"

He was done making eye contact. Instead, he pressed on the gas even harder.

I yanked the wheel and we veered off into the bar ditch, but only for a second because he was just as strong as I was, and he was determined not to let his mother's van be pulled over.

It was time to quit playing games. The clock was ticking. "Dude, you realize we need a plan, don't you? We can't just hightail it back over there and save the day."

"Says who?" Sonny yelled.

"Says me!"

He wasn't seeing what I considered to be the big, obvious reasons, which made it hard not to smack him upside the head.

I scoped out the area, trying to figure out who we knew that lived within a mile or two.

"I tell you what, you make a plan; I'll drive," Sonny said as he pointed to an imaginary wristwatch.

"You win, Dude. Now, who lives around here that we know?"

"Why?"

"Sonny, we need a gun before we go back there. You know that almost every home out in these parts has a gun in it. So who's closest? We can't go back to the Pachecos' unprepared."

He slammed the brakes right before the turnoff to their house.

"So much for not pulling over," I mumbled, trying not to sound too sarcastic.

Sonny banged his hand against the wheel hard enough that I fully expected it to bust. "Dammit, I don't wanna use a gun, Javen."

"Me neither. But I don't wanna lose this fucker again. Do you understand how that could happen if he has a gun and we don't?"

He mulled this over a good three seconds. "All right. I have a gun at home."

"So do I, Boy Wonder...a lot of good it's doing way over there. But let's just say your place was within a mile or two, which it isn't, you think you could get it and leave the house without anyone noticing?"

That was probably the first stupid question I'd ever asked that he didn't bother trying to answer.

I got out of the van, slammed my door harder than necessary and tried to calm myself down enough to think rationally. But there was too much going on in my head. I could feel my blood pulsing in my fingertips as I pressed them against one another, against my face, like I was praying. Only I wasn't. I was just trying to concentrate. But nothing was coming to me. Nothing but the sound of the wind picking up, gusting like a dirt devil was about to pass over us. Only there wasn't dirt flying. Just an old can. A can that made all sorts of noise as it tumbled across the road and stopped at my shoe. I bent over and picked it up, looked it over. It was an old can covered in holes, like someone had used it for target practice a million years ago.

Target practice. My God, why hadn't I thought of it before? Maybe it had been a prayer after all.

Sonny was out of the van by now. "So what's the genius plan you've concocted to save the day?"

I threw him the can. "*Concocted*? That's a big word, Dude. Don't hurt yourself."

He stood there holding it as I got back into the van.

"Let's go!" I yelled.

"Where to?" he asked as he got back in and tossed the can behind him.

"Joey's place. His house is, what, two miles south of here?"

"Hell no, I'm not ready to see Joey's family."

"Well get ready, Son. It's gotta be quick anyway. We're in a hurry, remember?"

"Why now?"

I gave him a full minute before filling the blanks in for him. "His dad's rifle is in the shed, behind the house...you know, back where we always shoot targets and —"

"And cans," he said, grinning wide.

Finally.

"Yeah. And cans."

Chapter 17
Sonny's Story

A blood blister had formed in the palm of my right hand sometime the day before. While inner-tubing, maybe. Or was it while I held the gun? None of it mattered anyhow. I just wanted it gone. And so I pinched it with my teeth, tryin' to get it to burst as we got closer and closer to the House of Sadness.

The closer we got, the more I needed the blister to explode. Bleed out. Disappear already. But it was as stubborn as a mole or a wart.

"So tell me again how we're pulling this off?" I asked.

"All right, listen up, Sonny. I'm just here to return Joey's bag. You with me so far?"

"Don't be a smartass."

"And since I know you don't have it in you to be brief for fear of coming off as rude, I'm gonna to do the honors of knocking at the door. Once inside, I'm gonna take all of five minutes. Meanwhile, you are gonna go get the gun."

"Yeah, but what if they see us pull up and then wonder where the hell I went."

"I'm dropping you off at the mailbox on the highway. You'll have to haul ass through the boondocks, open the shed, get the rifle and meet me back at the mailbox. That way nobody in that house sees anyone but me."

"And when they ask what you're doin' driving around in the minivan?"

"Gimme a break, Sonny. Do you really want me to count all the times I've driven this hunk o' junk? I can see it in the papers now: 'Javen Found Driving Goretti Minivan...again'."

It was good to know that yesterday hadn't changed everything. I could still count on him acting like an ass at the best of times.

"Why do we have to be all sneaky, Javen? I mean, why don't we just ask Mr. Diaz for the rifle? Maybe even bring him back with us while we're at it?"

"Dude, his son just died. You think he wants to deal with this bullshit? And, what, you don't think we can handle this?"

I wanted to say no, but I just shrugged my shoulders instead.

"So this is gonna take five minutes?"

He thought a minute here. "You're right. I forget you don't hold the title for world's fastest runner. Okay, eight minutes."

"*Eight*? Are you sure? Not eight and a half? Eight and three quarters?"

He sighed all heavy and sarcastic before pointing to his imaginary watch.

I laughed. "Fine. Eight minutes it is."

As I pulled up to the mailbox, Javen fished out a notebook from Joe's bag.

"What's that?" I asked.

"Nothing, just a notebook I lent him."

"*You* loaned a notebook to *Joey*?" Actually, the real mystery was why he wanted it back. But I let it go.

"All right, let's do this," he said.

I got out, van still runnin', and gave my blood blister one more unsuccessful nibble.

"See you in eight minutes, Sonny."

There was no dilly-dallying for my boy Javen. He didn't even say goodbye or take the time to prepare a speech before moving on. He just hit the gas and, before I knew it, I was choking on his dust. Which probably pissed him off. The fact that I wasted a good half minute standing there watching the ass of the van drive away.

While my heart and brain and stomach might have

hesitated, Javen evidently put the fear of God in my legs because I was standin' at the door of the shed in no time at all.

I needed to think about where I remembered seeing the rifle last. And then it came to me...it was in Mr. Diaz's lap. I remember I'd walked back there looking for Joey and found the both of them sittin' on a bench. Mr. Diaz was cleaning the gun. Joey was drinkin' a soda and watching.

"It's damn ugly, but it shoots pretty good, qué no?" Mr. Diaz was saying as I walked in.

"We need a high-powered scope, Papá. *Then* it'll shoot pretty good."

"*¿Para qué?*" he answered sarcastically. "To shoot the tails off of lizards?"

"No, but what if I ever have to shoot the face off a rattlesnake? When you're mano a mano with a rattler, losing isn't an option. ¿Qué no?"

I remember how he smiled, like he was proud of Joey's quick thinking. But Mr. Diaz needed to remind him that he didn't know everything. "Si encuetras con una víbora, la mira del rifle te va salir cola, mi'jo. All you will need is your quick thinking.

"But I tell you what, graduate con honores and I'll get your telescopio."

Well, he got the honors. But I'd'a been willing to bet a pretty penny that Joey had long forgotten about that stupid scope.

I opened the door to the shed and found the rifle immediately. There, sitting on that same bench was Mr. Diaz holding it. I must'a jumped back a whole ten feet. It was like someone had turned back the hands of time. Except for the bench. The space where Joey usually sat reminded me that this wasn't a time-traveling pleasure trip. That, and the emptiness in Mr. Diaz' face.

Suddenly, I wondered what he was doin' with the rifle in his lap. The only thing that crossed my mind made my heart skip a beat, maybe even two or three.

But he hadn't vacated after all because, somehow, he picked up on my thoughts, or maybe the panic in my eyes. "Don't worry, mi'jo. I'm just sitting here, wishing I had bought un chingao telescopio."

"Mr. Diaz, Joey needed that scope like he needed a hole..."

Oh my God, what the hell am I saying? It wasn't his head, but it was a hole. A hole he didn't need. I could never say that phrase ever again. Something else I couldn't do was come up with a quick save. Not even a lame one.

"Come sit down," he said.

The last thing I felt like doing was making myself comfortable on that bench. Joey's seat. And yet how could I be rude to Mr. Diaz? So I sat, my head feeling hot and heavy, like I got an instant case of flu.

"Do you know what this is?" he asked.

"A rifle?"

He laughed softly. "No, mi'jo. Qué tipo. What kind?"

"To be honest, I'd never paid it much attention."

"It's a Marlin 17V. I bought it at a flea market. Muy barata. Very cheap....

"But José was right. It needs a pinche scope. Excuse my language, mi'jo."

I watched the way he handled it, like he was petting a sleeping lap dog. "I don't know, Mr. Diaz. I've shot my fair share of rabbits using that thing. I think it does okay without a scope...you know, for what we used it for." I'd already forgotten what the hell I was doin' there.

Then Mr. Diaz held the gun up like he was gonna shoot and looked over the barrel that was pointed at the door. "You're right, mi'jo. If you just focus, you won't have a wild shot," he said, putting the gun back on his lap, petting it once more. "It's nothing fancy, but I'm pretty sure it could shoot the head off a rattlesnake. Facil."

"I guess it's lucky for us we never had to find out," I said. But luck was no better a subject to talk about than "holes in heads" was. I'd never wished for laryngitis so much in all my life. Something needed to make me shut up.

But Mr. Diaz and I weren't even on the same wavelength.

"No necesitó un telescopio. Yo se que no necesitó," he mumbled while I fixated on my luck comment.

Then he thrust out his arms and handed me the rifle. "Here, mi'jo. I can't look at this thing anymore."

For some reason, it felt a lot heavier than I remembered. Maybe it was the way he had handed it over to me, like a weightlifter dropping down his barbell.

"Quick and careful. Just remember that, mi'jo. Whenever you're in trouble, there's no time to be afraid. You just make sure to use it wisely."

"Okay," I said, but only because I didn't wanna stick my foot in my mouth anymore. Under a different set of conditions I might'a said, *'Quick and careful?' Those two words have never been used to describe me in my entire life.* So maybe this rifle is the last thing I need.

"Mr. Diaz —"

"Just...take it. And cuidado because it's loaded," he said.

I didn't know what to say besides, "Thank you."

Mr. Diaz walked to the door of the shed and then turned and looked straight at me. "Will you tell me why you came for the gun, mi'jo?"

My heart started jumping like crazy as I tried to think up a lie on the spot. It was no good. Everyone knew what old Santino was holding before Santino did. I didn't think that Mr. Diaz would believe me anyway.

"No, sir, I can't."

He considered that carefully and gave a quick nod. "Then you better get going. You don't want to keep Javen waiting." He turned back towards the door. "And remember to keep your eyes open for víboras. Sometimes those damn things don't rattle until it's too late."

Javen. It hadn't even occurred to me to question how he knew Javen was waiting. Mr. Diaz had always been smarter than people gave him credit for...well, not including Joey. That boy had his dad pegged from day one. I looked down at my blood blister, bared my teeth and gave it one more try. It finally popped. Effortlessly even.

Chapter 18
Antonia's Story

Until now, I hadn't noticed that my mother was still in her pajama top from the night before; her long-sleeved, collared flannel with the pink and red hearts, all wrinkly and stained with yesterday's coffee. She could have been mistaken for your average American mother on a late Saturday morning. Except that her face very clearly said *Life as I've known it is over.* Her expression was as beaten as our football field at the end of the season.

"It's missing," she said.

"What's missing?" Madrid asked.

Mom displayed the inside of the envelope like that would answer her question. When she realized that it didn't, she said, "My history...*our* history..."

"You mean the written record of it, Mom," I said. "It's not gone altogether."

"Did you take it, Madrid?"

It was as if she hadn't even heard me. I tried again. "Mom, you know all this. Weren't those papers just your backup?"

She walked to the foot of my bed and gently sat, as though I was still sleeping and she didn't want to wake me. "Yes. You're right. I just always thought...I always thought I would start this conversation with the picture...." She was still peering inside the envelope like something might magically appear if she looked long and hard enough. Then again, maybe she was just avoiding the issue — and my eyes. "Where could they be?" she whispered.

"You haven't seen them, Madrid?" she asked again, more exasperated than the first time. "My picture of the twins? The letter?"

Madrid hesitated a moment before answering. "I've only seen —"

"So you *do* have them. Thank God." She breathed an exaggerated sigh of relief.

"No, Mom. I saw a picture of twins...it was sticking out from under your mattress last Sunday, Mother's Day, when I made your bed for you. But I never saw a letter. Or that envelope."

"Madrid, this is where I kept them both! It was all under my mattress together. And now it's empty." Her voice was gaining momentum.

But so was Madrid's. "I didn't take anything! I never even picked up your mattress to see what else you had hiding under there, Mom." Her voice quivered a little as she continued to defend herself. "I just saw the picture. *That's all!*"

"All right, fine, let's just put the letter aside for now. I would still like the pic —"

"Mom, will you stop harassing her about the stupid picture already? Just let it go! All I want from you right now is an answer. Just one."

But Madrid wanted something, too...to claim her innocence once and for all. "I never took it out of your room. I just tucked it back under your mattress after I was done making the bed. Unless you've looked at it since then, it should still be there." She hadn't stuttered once in all my mother's grilling. My mother's procrastinating, actually. Mom didn't even notice. She didn't show any signs of noticing her crying, either, as Madrid rose to go look for the stupid picture, the one she'd tried telling me about earlier.

"No, I'll look." My mother rose to leave as well. But Madrid was already out the door before she even finished her sentence.

Mom had a gift for rousing action almost imperceptibly. Her assistants, in particular, toiled to make her look flawless in her position as superintendent, the women who tugged at their skirts when they thought her critical eye disapproved of the length. Who ran to the nearest bathroom and blotted at their lipstick when she'd comment on how "electricfying" their faces looked. They tried to please her because she rewarded their good behavior, if not with bonuses and time off, then with the little things...smiles, compliments, attention to the details of their lives. I suppose she did the same thing with us. But it had never felt so palpable. Or deliberate. I suddenly wondered if every kind gesture and act of generosity she had ever performed was calculated. She was manipulating the situation by doing everything in her power to avoid the real issue, by focusing on something as irrelevant as a picture. And taking it out on Madrid, no less. Did she really think I would put it aside? Get hungry, or sleepy, or just forget about it altogether if she spent enough time fixating on a photograph?

Yes. She did. It's what she always did. Only I wasn't going to let it happen anymore. "Why won't you look at me?"

Not even the question would make her look at me, much less dignify it with an answer. Instead, her eyes drilled a hole right through an arbitrary place somewhere near her lap as we waited for Madrid's return.

Linda Rondstadt started singing "Por Un Amor" from my stereo. "For a Love." It was a song from her first Mexican music CD, my mother's favorite and, incidentally, something I'd never taken out of its case, much less brought into my room. I barely recognized what it was because it was playing so low you had to strain to hear it. Just as I realized what that fact implied, the volume gradually began to rise until it was unbearably loud. I checked for the sake of practicality, to see if I had sat on the remote. Mom did the same.

I walked over to the stereo to turn it down, and the volume began to steadily fall as I approached it. I stopped in my tracks, the volume steadily rose again. Down. Up. Down. And, still, I couldn't persuade myself to turn around and face the room now that I knew Adolph was in it.

"You do realize she's never going to get to the truth, don't you, Antonia?"

I waited for him to lower the volume before turning around.

Madrid's was the first face I saw. She and Adolph stood at the doorway of my bedroom. He had her arms pinned behind her back. Her fear-stricken face couldn't disguise her pain as she struggled to free herself.

I wanted to go to her, comfort her, tell her that everything was going to be okay. But, even if I thought Adolph would allow it, the gun he had pointed at Madrid's head stopped me cold.

"I'll ask you the same question that you just asked your mother — 'Why won't you look at me?'" he said as he released my sister. Madrid backed into the corner of my room and covered her face with her hands.

I brushed the bangs from my forehead and looked directly into his eyes.

He appeared identical to how I'd last seen him in the forest — dirty, sweaty, ominous. Only his face was now very bruised and swollen. His left thumb was casually hooked at the pocket of his shorts, a revolver cradled in his right palm. He was smiling the same smile, the one that I trusted what felt like a thousand years ago. Like I trusted Mom's virtue. And Joey's promise. And Javen's guarantee that everything was going to be all right.

"That's my girl," he said. "Now I can see those gray eyes that know me so well."

"You're revising history, Adolph. You're the one who knows *me* so well. Remember?"

He threw his head back and laughed at this. "If only you knew how well.

"But speaking of knowing me, Madrid and I met out in the hallway. Isn't that right, Madrid."

Madrid was shaking so much it was impossible to tell that she was nodding.

"Aw, Sweetheart. It's okay. No need to be so fearful. In fact, why don't you come back and stand over here by me."

She quickly lifted her head from her hands and looked at me for rescuing words. But in my own panic, I had none for her.

Adolph laid the remote down on my dresser and limped over to where she was standing. "It's all right. I'll just come to you...such a pretty girl."

Madrid was still looking at me, whimpering, as Adolph put an arm around her trembling shoulder and guided her closer to my bed.

"Antonia..." My mother's voice tugged at me. It said *Look at me...I'm here now...I'm with you....* Her eyes said the same thing. Finally.

"What do we need to do for this young man," she continued.

"I don't need a thing, Mom," he answered for me. "On the other hand, Madrid here looks like she could use a drink. Or a hug maybe? Come here, Sweetie." Adolph hugged her deep, rubbing her back sensuously, the gun pressing into her skin.

"Please, no," Madrid cried almost too softly to hear.

"You're scaring her!" Mom scolded. Tugging at Madrid's hand.

"Adolph!" Now I was the one tugging.

He quit hugging Madrid and looked at me eagerly.

The moment he let go of her, Mom seized the opportunity to yank her back. But Adolph was much quicker, even in his weakened state. His gun landed squarely against the right side of my mother's head. Madrid screamed loud enough for the three of us.

"I'm okay, I'm okay," she said while trying to shield the sight of blood with her hand. It was only meant to reassure

Madrid because I knew she was in serious pain. The sound of the impact said it all. She was unsteady as she bit down on her lip and furrowed her brows, her eyes tightly shut.

Adolph laughed as he watched me pull the corner of my comforter out and press it against my mother's wound.

Things were only bound to get worse if I didn't turn his attention back to me.

"You're right, Adolph. I do know you pretty well. I know that you didn't just come here for a friendly visit."

A smile began to spread across his face. "All right, so why did I come here?"

"You came here for me."

He thought about my answer for a moment. "I think you can do better than that."

"If you don't mind, I'll spare my family the graphics."

Adolph walked over to my desk chair and slowly pulled it over. If his face didn't say so, then the methodic way he situated himself made it obvious that he was still in pain from the beating the night before. "Go and have a seat next to your mother, Madrid."

I scooted over to make room for her just as she jumped on the bed and threw her arms around my bleeding mother. Mom held her tight as Adolph gently crossed one leg over the other and put his arms behind his head. The gun was now resting on his belly.

"Oh, Antonia...I wasn't asking for graphics. Don't you see? We are more alike than you realize."

"I am *nothing* like you."

He put his arms down and bent forward after moving the gun from his belly and let it hang between his legs.

"Just for kicks, Antonia, tell us how many times we touched over at the hot springs."

I knew the answer. The fact that I knew, just *that* quick creeped me out.

He laughed. "Go ahead. You can say it."

It crossed my mind to lie and say I didn't know, but I couldn't risk his anger.

"Six."

"Are you sure?"

"Yes."

"Oh my God," Madrid whispered.

"Pretty impressive, huh? Tell me, Antonia, quick, how many nightmares have you had in the last month?"

"You told him about your nightmares?" my mother asked.

"No!"

"Mind your business, Felicia!

"To think about it is to cheat, Antonia. An answer. Quick!"

My mind went back to the hospital and Joey dying. Back farther, to the moment when Joey was shot. Back to the moment when we held hands at dusk and he began to recite his poem. Back to the river and all that time spent searching. Sitting next to Joey on that rock as we fed a chipmunk.... Holding his hand as we walked from the hot springs back to camp. My heart was now wedged in my throat as I remembered the warmth of his hand. I went all the way back to the moment when Joey and Adolph yanked me in opposite directions....

"You've read my journal."

Adolph looked bored as he considered the accusation.

"Do you know how many little girls I've killed, Antonia?" he asked indifferently.

"How many dreams?"

"You already know."

"That is not the point of this exercise."

"Then what is? To prove that I'm as creepy as you are? I haven't *murdered* anyone, Adolph!"

"How many?"

"I don't know!"

"Five, six, pick up sticks...."

"Six! Seven!" I shouted. Then hesitated.

"Adolph," I whispered. "Why are you here?"

He smiled and turned to Madrid, the gun now hung loosely from his right hand. "I love this girl," he said to her.

"I want you to tell them why I'm here, Antonia."

I sighed in frustration. "If I had to guess, I'd say you're only here to have a little fun with my family before you have some fun with me. Because God knows we're soulmates, right? But then you'll realize that I'm a lousy lay because I don't fight and scream and bleed quite right, so you'll have to fix that."

"That's very good, Antonia. Very good. But...disappointingly wrong. Partially wrong anyway. You see, *God* knows nothing of the sort. I could never be soulmates with someone as filthy as you. But here's what I can do...I can sit back and watch the roaches scurry as I spray them with Raid. Watch them squirm as they try to escape, their filthy bodies wet with the toxins frying their brains, twitching... always twitching.... And they still try to get away, don't they?" He looked at me like a disapproving father.

"Dying shouldn't frighten people Antonia. It's a liberating experience."

He glanced at Madrid and my mother. "I'm going to set you two free."

"Stop it, Adolph. You're going to kill us all! Just say it!"

"You're wrong Antonia. I can only set one person on that path at a time. Counting is like that...one, two, buckle my shoe...three, four, close the door..." he started humming the nursery rhyme and smiled, like a child reprieved from harsh punishment.

"They'll miss you Antonia, might even go insane if they watch as I set you free. They won't understand my purpose — won't see the transcendent beauty. They'll fixate instead on the transient ugliness.

"But rest assured it's not their time. It's not their time to die."

I knew he was telling the truth. I didn't know how I knew but....

He turned to my mother. "I'm not sure exactly what I expected out of you today.... I suppose I was testing your parenting skills under conditions of duress. Not surprisingly, you have failed before we've even begun."

God forbid anyone call Mom's parental skills into question. "I'm not sure what you mean, but we are at the mercy of your weapon, Mr..."

"Mister is fine for now. The point is that you, like most of your kind, are a liar. And I hypothesize that you will not tell the truth. Not even now, with someone willing to use a gun to get the truth out of you."

"I've changed my mind, Adolph. I don't want an explanation from her anymore." In the silence that followed, Madrid's whimpering sounded abnormally loud. I wanted her to stop. It was just the kind of disruption that could make him kill.

He didn't seem to notice. "This isn't about you, Antonia."

"Then what the hell is it about?" Madrid blurted out.

Mom placed her hand over Madrid's mouth and I apologized for her, over and over, until Adolph put his hand up in the air for me to stop.

"Actually, I appreciate her honesty."

"And just who the hell are you to judge anyone's honesty. I trusted you...told you things...and you never let on what you were planning."

"Yes. I did. Eventually I did. Don't you remember? I told you that it was you I really wanted."

"Now you have the audacity to judge my mother for her own lie? At least my mother hasn't killed anyone!"

"That's true...but *you* have."

"Don't!" Mom yelled. "Not like this."

"Oh, don't worry, Mom. I have no intention of doing your job for you." He pulled out a thick roll of legal paper from his waistband at the small of his back. "Do you need this to refresh your memory?"

"No," she quickly said. "No. I don't."

"So maybe I should give it to Antonia? That way she can follow along while you recite your lines." He made like he was going to hand me the papers when Mom jerked forward and made a grab for them.

The gun was instantly at her head. "No quick movements, okay, Mom?

Mom looked at me long and hard. Then turned back to Adolph.

The gun would no longer be a token of authority. It was obvious that he planned to have it pointed at my mother for the duration of her confession.

He moved closer to my mom and pressed his gun to her head. "How your daughter must hate you, Felicia," he said, glancing at me. "Your selfishness, your betrayal."

He whispered in her ear. "You'll see that hatred in her eyes when I set her free."

Along with the thick bundle of yellow paper was the picture. Adolph examined it one last time, shaking his head and smirking, before handing it over to me.

It's funny, but I wasn't the least bit curious about that thing. Not even a little. I had already seen Stacia, after all. That picture was as useless to me now as my hand on Joey's wound turned out to be yesterday.

But then I saw it — the crinkly-soft paper, our small bodies wrapped in yellow crocheted blankets and the man, whom I presumed was Matthew, holding us both.

"Why?" I cried out.

My mother recoiled as the shrillness of my voice shook the room. "Why didn't I tell you?"

"No! Why did you make me forget them?"

She opened her mouth and then looked at Adolph in desperation, at the gun pointing at her. "I don't...."

"How about this, Felicia — just don't." He lowered the gun. "You can stay here with Madrid. And live."

"What about Antonia?" Madrid asked, not realizing that this wasn't even remotely close to a merciful freebie.

"Just give me a moment," Mom pleaded.

"You've had, what, fifteen years worth of moments, Mom? And now you have the impudence to ask for one more?" He contorted his face in pain as he stood to leave. "Let's go, Antonia."

"No!" Madrid shouted.

"You explain to me how a mother tells her three-year-old, or five-year-old, or twelve-year-old...when is a good age to tell your daughter that she is responsible for the death of her own twin sister?" Mom clasped her hands to her mouth, but it was too late.

"So it's true," I whispered.

"Yes, it's true, Baby," she whispered back.

"How can you say that?" Madrid yelled, letting go of my mother's hand.

"Why else would I move you both so far away from home? Why else would I lie to you? Live without the memory of my Stacia?" She turned her attention back toward me. "Your twin sister."

I looked at Madrid. "You didn't know?"

She shook her head fervently.

"Nobody around here knew anything...except Joey's mother. She was the only person I confided in. I shouldn't have spoken to *anyone*. I didn't want you to know before it was time. I didn't want you to ever find out accidentally. But I had to talk to somebody."

"What did she do?" Madrid asked softly.

"Don't...." Mom begged. Her lips trembled at the thought of saying the words. "It was just an accident, mi'ja, a completely innocent accident."

"What did I do, Mom? Will you please just say it?"

She'd quit holding my comforter to her head. She'd finally regained her equilibrium as well. She was perfectly lucid when she said the words I'd waited fifteen years to hear. "You accidentally shot and killed your twin sister Stacia while she was sleeping."

"There. Now was that so hard?" Adolph asked. "But you aren't done. Tell her how it wasn't just a lie by omission. Tell her how it was a lie in the truest sense of the word. Tell her about the fire."

"There was obviously no fire," Mom said with an exasperated sigh.

"So then what happened to our dad?" Madrid asked.

Mom didn't answer.

"That's your cue, Felicia."

"Please!"

Wrong answer. Before she could change her mind and give him the right one, Adolph put a bullet hole through my stereo and, again, hit my mom against the side of her head with the butt of his gun.

Madrid screamed as Mom crumpled to the floor and frantically tried to stop the flow of blood that streamed from the gash on the side of her head.

Adolph considered the two of them for a moment before turning back to me.

"You're better off without her, Antonia."

I stood paralyzed. I had no control over my body.

Adolph looked directly into my eyes and caressed my cheek lightly. His touch brought chills to the surface.

"You *were* attracted to me back at the springs, weren't you?" he whispered against my ear.

I didn't answer.

He pulled away from my face so I could better see his darkened expression. "Don't lie to me, Antonia. I won't be lied to."

I gasped in pain as his hand twisted in my hair.

I didn't want to believe it, but it was true. I had been attracted to him — or to the person I thought he was. I told myself that it was only because I was feeling lonely and sorry for myself that I even talked to him, but I knew it wasn't true. I didn't see past his looks, his clean scent, his fake openness. The person I thought I was attracted to never really existed.

I turned to look at Madrid cradling my mom's head in her lap and sobbing softly. I couldn't tell if she was conscious or not. It was strange. I'd just learned that I killed my twin sister. The details were still fuzzy, and yet all I could think about was how to stop Adolph from taking my mother and younger sister away from me, too. I loved them so much. I fought back tears as I realized that I hadn't told them so nearly enough. Now it was too late.

Adolph twisted my arm behind my back. "Say it, Antonia. You were attracted to me, weren't you?"

"No," I whispered, bracing myself for the pain.

"You truly disappoint me, you know that?"

"Where do we go from here, Adolph?" I asked.

But did I really want to know? If his goal was to kill me, why all this agony? If I was just gonna die anyway, why was he investing so much time into getting my mother to fess up about my past?

Before my mind could come up with a list of possible reasons, I heard the washroom door squeak open...*maybe I'm the only one that heard it*, I thought, just before it became evident that I wasn't.

"Who's here with us?" Adolph said to no one in particular.

"Nobody. The kitchen window is open. The wind sometimes makes the squeaky washroom door sway," I said. I even had myself half convinced, even though I knew that it would take quite a gust of wind to move that heavy door.

"Why should I believe you?"

"Because I wouldn't risk a lie at a time like this."

"Is that so? On page 28 of your journal, you state that your belief in your mother's ability to tell the truth is dying. *Dying*, Antonia. You use the word dying. How...appropriate, don't you think?" His eyes narrowed, "It's my guess that the apple doesn't fall too far from the tree."

The squeak. It was louder this time. Definitely not the wind. My heart wanted to believe it was Joey.

Chapter 19
Javen's Story

I had no idea where we were even supposed to begin looking. The Pacheco house wasn't a shack by any means. He could be anywhere — the horse corrals, the garage, the shed, the bushes lying just outside the fields of alfalfa.... Worse case scenario: he was already with them.

If I was going to do this right, I had to believe that Joey was here, that the can had been more than just a heads-up, that not even death would keep him away at a time like this. It wasn't about avenging his killer or trying to be a hero. We were a team. We helped each other. Joey wouldn't think it was an option to skip out on us any more than I would have in his shoes. Maybe Sonny would've. Nah, not even Sonny.

"So do you have any great ideas up your sleeve?" he asked.

"No, and we're pretty much out of time to think one up," I said as I turned left onto the dirt road leading directly to their driveway. I slowed way down to cut back on the noise and dust, and then I parked about fifty yards from the front door.

"We're here," I said.

Sonny started to breathe like a football player about to run onto the field.

"Calm down, Sonny."

"I'm calm. I'm calm. I'm calm," he chanted.

"Good, I believe you. I believe you. I believe you."

Once he got his breathing under control, the shakes

and heavy sweating started. It was a sad thing, but nobody thought less of Sonny than Sonny. There was this book, *Pooh's Grand Adventure*, that I always used to read to his youngest sister. In the book, Christopher Robin says to Pooh that he's braver than he believes, and stronger than he seems, and smarter than he thinks. If it wasn't so fucking corny, I would have passed this information along to Sonny right now.

"So what do you say we go in through the kitchen?" I asked, trying to get him to relax a little.

"Why the kitchen?"

"Well, you could grab a bite for yourself and make a ham sandwich for me while you're —"

I quit when I realized he wasn't in the mood for humor.

"All right, here's why: Because something tells me Adolph wouldn't be in such an open area where he'd have to keep his eye on, like, three different doorways. And, besides that, they always keep the kitchen door unlocked, so we can just let ourselves in."

"Much better answer."

"And how does this sound...once we get in, I'll head straight for the laundry room and wait there for you to check things out." I was completely making this up as I went along. "If all's clear, you come back and let me know. If not, I come out and start firing."

He was just as unconvinced that my plan was gonna work as I was. But he didn't put a better plan on the table, either. "All right. Just remember, that room has a squeaky door, and we need to be extra quiet in case what's-his-face is in the house, Jav."

"You just hurry your ass up and see that they're all right while I'm in there. And do it quietly."

"I'm not making any promises."

I thumped the side of his head. "And when you see that they're all right, you come right back out and we'll start searching the whole place."

"So tell me again what happens if he is in there? I

mean, how the hell are you supposed to know?"

"I'll give you two minutes."

"Dude, let's not get into the time thing again."

"Then you make sure you hurry your ass up so that I don't start to panic."

"What if we're too late?"

"Then your hitchhiker was nothing more than one sick dude."

"He wasn't."

"That's right. So let's go already."

I knew just by the way he grabbed the bag the hitchhiker had given him that he was feeling braver now. He opened it up and pulled out a red t-shirt and rope.

"What the hell's that?"

"I already told you. A present."

"And just what are you supposed to do with it?"

He laid the nylon rope on the dashboard while he put the red t-shirt on.

"Eddie told me that a team has a better chance of winning when they're wearing red. You think it's true?"

"Maybe," I said as sincerely as I could. "But why the hell couldn't you have told me you read it in *Sports Illustrated* or something? 'Cause the second I hear it came out of Eddie's mouth, I automatically chalk it up to bullshit."

Sonny looked like he was second-guessing himself for a minute there, but only for a minute. "Today, it's true, all right? Besides, I don't know what else I'm supposed to do with a t-shirt."

I didn't know, either. Nor did I care. I grabbed the gun, and we made like a couple of chicken thieves creeping up to the hen house. I pulled the door open a crack and looked around.

"Now remember, Sonny, you need to make this quick," I said once we were inside and it was obvious that no one was in the kitchen or living room.

"I know," he hissed. "Let's go already."

I pulled the laundry room door shut behind me, every muscle in my body tied up in a knot anticipating the squeak. But it didn't come, not even a little. Who knows for sure, but maybe that was our first favor from Joey.

Once in there, I wondered why I bothered shutting the stupid door in the first place.

As I strained to listen, I could hear Ms. Pacheco's voice, but only barely. I could tell that they were down the hall in Antonia's bedroom. It sounded like everything was okay. Just as I let relief settle in, I heard a guy's voice. A guy's voice that didn't belong to Sonny. And, while I was sure that Joey was with us somehow, I knew that wasn't his voice I was hearing, either. No cars were parked outside. There were no neighbors close enough to walk over. It was Adolph's voice. He had beaten us.

I stayed real still, even held my breath. Where was Sonny? Gunless, fucking Sonny. I had to open the door and check things out.

My muscles tensed up all over again as I tried to think fast, tried to figure out the best way to not mess things up by opening the door that was sure to squeak this time. And then a gun shot rang out, so loud that it shook the windows. My first reaction was to charge out of there full speed. But I'd already seen what Adolph was capable of, and so I held back for a minute. I waited for voices. There was Madrid's scream, then Antonia's voice. Relief. Sweet relief.

I gave the door a gentle push. Sure enough. *Squeak.* I stopped pushing before it opened more than an inch and listened again. There was that deceiving moment of silence before Adolph's freak-out, the moment when I foolishly thought that everything might be cool for just a bit longer.

Where's Sonny, and what the hell is he doing? Why isn't he whispering at me through the door, bitching about my plan getting all screwed up?

My impatience was getting the best of me. Besides, it was time to get out and hide somewhere else before Adolph came back and followed the squeak. I opened the door full-force, tiptoed as quick as I could into the living room, hiding on the side of the couch furthest from the hallway. I looked around for Sonny. He was nowhere to be seen. And sure as shit, Adolph came out with Madrid to check out the second, much louder squeak.

"Remember, if either of you move, Madrid will quickly become a thing of the past."

He held her around the waist, gun to the back of her head as she walked in front of him. They were headed straight for the squeaky door. In a few seconds, he would see that nobody was there. Maybe he would pull up the blinds and see the van. Maybe that would cause him to shoot Madrid. I had to get him first. But I hadn't even made sure the round was chambered. And hell if I would bluff it. I was going to make noise checking. I needed to do it somewhere other than the living room. Antonia's closet, maybe.

As soon as he was in the laundry room, I made a beeline to the bedroom. As I passed Madrid's bedroom, a rope came flying out at me.

What the hell does he want me to do with this?

I cursed Sonny for distracting me as I kept sprinting toward the bedroom.

When I ran in, Antonia gasped. Ms. Pacheco was bleeding pretty bad and looked out of it. I ran into Antonia's walk-in closet, where I closed the door and turned on the light to inspect the rifle.

"Turn it off," Antonia whispered loud enough for me to hear. So I did, without a second thought.

"Come out, come out, wherever you are!" Adolph bellowed as he walked back toward the bedroom.

There was scuffling, a loud thud, and another shot. And I knew. Oh God, I knew.

"Javen!" Sonny screamed.

I couldn't get out quick enough. I tripped over Antonia's shoes. Antonia pulled me up from the floor and I ran into the hallway, and there was Joey's second favor — Madrid on the ground looking up at the hole in the ceiling, Adolph lying on top of her.

"The rope!" Sonny screamed.

Sonny had his knee pressed into the middle of Adolph's back. He was holding Adolph's wrists together like the cops do in the movies just before the cuffs are latched on. But Adolph was strong.

It was a good thing Sonny threw me the rope. He'd've never been able to grow a third arm quick enough to actually put it to use. I came down and tried to tie Adolph's hands together, one still holding fast to his gun.

"The rifle!" Sonny yelled. Panic shot through me as Adolph struggled to get loose.

Where the hell had I laid it down? Third favor — right next to Sonny's right hand.

"Get Madrid out first!" Antonia shouted.

Sonny reached over and grabbed the rifle. Antonia was yanking on Madrid by her right arm, and I was trying to pry Adolph's gun from his hand. But the rope was nowhere near tight enough. Neither was the grip I had on him. The second Sonny went for the rifle, Adolph's right arm was freed. His fist and gun hit me in the temple so fast that I was blinded by stars and pain before I even realized what had happened.

There were two shots. And pain in my ears. Then screaming and a splatter of blood, I couldn't feel anything besides the pain in my head. I was pretty sure I hadn't been hit. I rubbed my eyes, and the image right in front of me slowly came into focus.

Sonny slumped against the wall. "Quick and careful," he was whispering. "He said to be quick and careful."

It was hard to tell where Sonny was bleeding from, what with his shirt being red. Antonia ran to him and tried to yank it off. He screamed in pain. And so she just held his head, like she'd held Joey's.

No sound came from Adolph. Not even a sigh. The back of his head was bleeding. He probably didn't have a mouth anymore.

"You see?" Sonny whispered. "There's something about

red uniforms. The hitchhiker dude knew."

"Yeah, Sonny. He knew."

"And so did Eddie."

"So maybe Eddie isn't the complete idiot I had him pegged for."

"Is he dead?" Madrid asked.

"Yes," Antonia said. "It's over. For now."

Chapter 20
Antonia's Story

Madrid and I sang our best rendition of John Jacob Jingleheimer Smith to distract Sonny while Javen applied first aid as we waited on the paramedics. Mom had regained consciousness but was still pretty unsteady as Javen and I tended to her. An embarrassed Mr. Fuentes turned up just after the ambulance. As it turned out, Adolph's dead body was wanted in five different states for eight other murders.

When the dust settled, Javen and Sonny were cleared of any suspicion. And the house was back in our possession.

As we waited in yet another hospital lobby, this time for Madrid to return with good word about yet another wounded friend, I finally got my answers.

"Did it happen the same day I had an operation?"

"Yes," Mom said. She was heavily bandaged and still groggy from the blows to her head.

All of us were examined when we got to the hospital and, aside from a few bumps and bruises, Madrid, Javen, and I checked out fine. The doctors were more worried about Mom, though. The hospital staff wanted to keep her overnight for observation, but Mom being Mom, she refused to be separated from her daughters.

"Stacia died the day you had your appendix taken out." Mom explained. The doctor said he'd never seen appendicitis occur at such a young age. That's what the scar on your belly is really about."

"Why'd you have to lie about that?" I asked without accusation.

"I thought if you remembered the appendicitis, you would surely have memories of Stacia dying since it all happened together, that same night."

The hippie was right. Hearing the truth felt very, very satisfying. Wires were untangling and reconnecting deep within my brain at an amazing rate.

"I remember," I said.

"You remember the appendicitis?" Javen asked.

"Well, I didn't know what it was. But I remember getting the pain in my stomach. I hunched forward and squeezed the trigger."

"You mean *pain* is what caused you to squeeze the trigger?" Mom asked incredulously.

I nodded.

She stared into space. "My God, all these years...I thought the appendicitis was an act of God to prevent you from remembering. I thought that God, in all his mercy, preoccupied you with the pain so you would forget the gun accident. I thought if you spent your time focused on healing, then maybe you would put the accident behind you...I had it so wrong."

She did have it all wrong. Because I missed her. I missed Stacia. I missed her while I was in the hospital and while Mom was trying to load us all up to move. Even when I didn't know what I was missing anymore, I missed her. The appendicitis did nothing to make me forget. *Mom* did that.

But I didn't need any more apologies. I just needed to put it all together so that I could let it go once and for all.

"I remember Matthew being there at the hospital with me," I said.

"Yes, he was. He held your hand all the way to the operating room. And sang —"

"John Jacob Jingleheimer Smith," we said in unison.

For the first time since the last time, my mother tried to hold me. And I let her.

"None of this was your fault, mi'jita. You were just a

child. It wasn't your fault my sister had a gun in the house. It was all just a terrible accident."

"I know," I said. And I really did. I turned to Javen, who was now sitting next to Madrid. I hadn't realized she was already back from visiting with the Gorettis, and I had no idea how much she had heard. Evidently, it was enough to make her throw her arms around me at the slightest invitation to come over by me.

"How's Sonny?" I asked.

"Well, he's going to live...if Mr. and Mrs. Goretti don't kill him when he gets back home."

"Yeah, his mom scoured this whole town looking for that boy, didn't she?" Javen said.

"Everywhere but the obvious place," Madrid said. "Thank God."

"Are they letting us lowlifes in his room yet?" Javen asked Madrid.

"Only immediate family," she said.

"That would be me." Javen stood to leave. "If you'll excuse me for a moment, I'm gonna go check in on our hero."

Now that my mother had told me the truth, it was time that I did the same.

"You aren't the only one that kept a secret, Mom." I braced myself for more of her pain. "Your sister died."

"How do you know?" she asked.

"You got an anonymous letter three years ago saying she had committed suicide. I never told you because at first I didn't think it was true, but then —"

"Mi'ja, it's okay. I know. Jewel told me. And I won't lie, it was hard to deal with. But, as both of you know, expressing our feelings has been such a taboo in this house...for all of us."

"*Had* been, Mom," Madrid said.

"Had been," she repeated.

"Why didn't you tell us that Jewel was our grandma?" Madrid asked. "And where's Matthew?"

"Mí Madrid...you've always been the quiet truth-seek-er. But you haven't unearthed everything, Sweetheart."

"What else is there?"

"Well...Jewel is Antonia's grandmother. But not yours." Mom sighed. "It's a very long story."

"Am I adopted?"

"Of course not!"

I laughed. "Madrid, you are the spitting image of Mom."

"Yeah, but then..."

"Sweetie, your dad is not Matthew. You are named after your dad, Madrid Pacheco. He and I were high school sweethearts. I married him very young. Too young, in fact." She took some tissues from her purse and wiped at her nose. "I loved him very much. But he was well on his way to being an alcoholic as young as fifteen. It was something that had always been socially acceptable to friends and family because he wasn't a belligerent drunk. And he was a good man in many other respects.

"But drinking became the most important thing in his life. And with every year that passed, I was drifting into a more permanent state of unhappiness. By the time I started graduate school, it was there to stay." She shook her head remembering.

"Anyway, I had classes at the university with Matthew. He stepped in and gave me the emotional support I needed. He was someone I felt myself falling in love with.

"We had an affair that ended in my getting pregnant.

"I suppose I could have lied and told your dad that the twins were his. But I made the decision to be honest about it. And he made the decision to forgive me. He promised to help me raise my babies and to quit drinking permanently. We were going to start over. And so I told Matthew that it was over. I wanted to make my marriage work.

"And we did. Well, we tried. Pretty soon you were born. I named you Madrid as a testament to my commitment. But the night that you came, he died in a car accident — hit a tree going about sixty miles an hour. He was killed instantly. His sobriety ended in a celebration for the birth of his baby girl.

"After that, parenthood felt the way a kidney must feel when its counterpart has been removed, like it has a responsibility to survive in order for the entire system to keep from shutting down. To me, that included keeping the truth from you."

"How did Matthew feel about the gun accident?" I asked.

"He was devastated, of course. Like we all were."

"Did you tell him you were leaving?"

"I didn't tell anyone. I left a note on my dad's pickup's windshield. I asked him to tell Matthew. It was a cruel thing to do...to everyone involved.

"At the time I just didn't think I had a choice. You could never accidentally learn about what happened. My baby had just died. In retrospect, I just wasn't thinking clearly."

"Matthew has never looked for us?"

"I don't know. I think he's trying to do what's right."

"When did you meet Jewel?" Madrid asked her.

"Well, she searched me out because of you guys. And she found me...she wanted to have a connection with her grandkids."

"You mean grandkid," Madrid said.

"No." Mom squeezed Madrid's hand. "That's not how she feels about it."

"What about her...did she know about the gun accident?" I asked.

"Yes. I told her. But she's a mother, too. She made no judgments about my decisions. She completely empathized."

"So how did Jewel know about your sister?" Madrid asked.

"Her name was Alicia, and Jewel had heard the news from Matthew. He'd seen her obituary in the newspaper and called my Mama to find out what happened. That's when they told him she'd killed herself."

"Why did she kill herself?" Madrid asked.

"Well...I think it's because she felt responsible for Stacia's death. And for my leaving town. I don't think she ever got over that. The accident happened on New Year's Eve. I had been invited to a party my cousin was throwing. Alicia offered to babysit you guys." Mom shook her head again, slower, sadder.

"I knew she was anxious about being alone since someone had recently broken into her apartment and robbed her blind. I had no business going to that party! But my cousin begged and begged and, like so many other times in my life, I didn't know how to say no."

"It's okay, Mom," Madrid offered, hugging her.

"Anyway, I thought she'd feel safer babysitting at our house. As it turned out, she didn't. I wish she'd have told me. Had I known that fear had prompted her to bring a gun along..."

"Mom, did she have a gap between her teeth?"

"Yes, you remember that?"

"I'm embarrassed to admit this, but she scared me. When I remember her face, I feel afraid.... Maybe it's because I remember her screaming and running out of the house with me...I'm sorry, there's no point in doing this."

"The point is to let it all out," Madrid said. "And, at the very least, to educate me. Because, unlike *you*, I was way too young to remember anything."

"Madrid, you aren't stuttering!"

Finally, my mother noticed.

Chapter 21
Javen's Story

I had gone to one graduation in my life before this one. It had been a cousin's, four years before. I remember there being lots of people who wouldn't sit down, wouldn't shut up, wouldn't walk away with their crying babies. This one wasn't much different. As I walked up to the podium and looked out to the audience, Joey's speech clutched in my sweaty hands, I didn't remember ever seeing as many people as I did at this particular one. There were people lined up standing at the very top of the bleachers. There were people leaning against the front fence separating the bleachers from the football field. There were people on top of people. You'd've thought an A-list celebrity was walking up there instead of me.

A week earlier, after Joey's funeral was over and I finally got to the familiar comfort of Sonny's hall bathroom where I could read that piece of paper in Joey's notebook, I realized it was his graduation speech. I read it to Ms. P over the phone and asked her what I should do with it.

"How would you feel about reading it for him? I think his words would mean a lot to everyone, especially his close friends and family," she said. I agreed. I decided to do it for Joey. I also decided it would probably be a good idea if I didn't look up while speaking, so I wouldn't get any more nervous than I absolutely had to.

Things started out pretty bad. Sonny and Antonia announced that I would be reading Joey's speech for him, making some comment about how I was his good friend, how Joey would be honored to have me speak on his behalf.

I'm not sure what else they were saying. I couldn't think, much less hear straight. The clapping started and I knew time was up. As I walked through the aisle, passing the two empty chairs with black ribbons around them for Joey and Dolores, I wondered if I looked like an ape. I wondered if my mother was watching...if Joey was watching. I wondered if I could do this without flinching, without showing my sadness over him not being here to do it himself.

As I started to speak, the microphone started screeching, so I backed up, but then I was too far away. It took what felt like thirty minutes to adjust the microphone to the right height before Ms. Pacheco, who sat behind me, walked up and helped me out. Before walking back to her seat, she squeezed my shoulders and whispered, "Just take a deep breath. Go slow. You'll be fine, mi'jo."

So I did. I inhaled deep and exhaled even deeper. I did feel better. But I think it had more to do with her words than with the breathing. I reopened the moist paper in my hand and began reading Joey's words:

"My friends have always said that I can tell a pretty good story. But what do you say to the class that thinks it's seen it all, heard it all, and knows it all already? Well, if you're José Diaz, you tell the truth as you know it. You also do your best to make it as short as possible so you won't lose your audience."

I looked over at Antonia and Sonny. Sonny gave me a thumbs-up. Antonia winked at me. I sighed real deep and continued to read aloud:

"There is a day in the back of my memory that stands out above the rest.

"I was on a fishing trip in the Gila forest with my family when I was eight years old. I'm sure I don't have to tell most of you what a beautiful place the Gila is, surrounded with mystery hiding not only in the walls of the cliff

dwellings, but in the whisper of the trees and the soil, the
river and the wildlife.

"It was there I learned that an uncle I never got to know
drowned while being forced to learn how to swim. I learned
that he was someone who wanted to grow up to be an
American farmer, and that my dad had witnessed his
brother's death at the hands of his own stepfather. For the
first time in my life, I was educated about true suffering,
about pain that wasn't physical in nature.It was the pain of
my father's memory."

I broke my rule and looked out at the audience.
Unbelievably, I found my mother. She was leaning up
against the fence, right next to me. Her cheerful pink
blouse was what caught my attention. She was by herself.
And she was crying. It caught me off guard. I'd never seen
her look so sad. I assumed it was for someone else, probably her husband, that guy I used to call Dad. I had to think
that in order to snap back and continue Joey's speech
where I'd left off. I might've driven myself crazy with questions otherwise. Questions like, "Why now?"

"Thankfully, I have yet to feel that kind of pain, so
maybe I'm not qualified to say what I'm about to say. But
today, I'm Joey Diaz, valedictorian, and so I'm going to say
it anyway.

"The good, the bad, the indifference, whatever you're
feeling right now — it's all due to your memories. You have
memories of looking into the mirror and seeing a man or
woman emerging. You have memories of dancing so close to
a girl or boy that you feel every part of your body ignite like
an oily cotton ball under a lit match. Memories of cruising
down a highway with your closest friends, just taking in
what it's like to be seventeen.

"But you also have memories of losing your favorite
grandmother or maybe the family you never even knew you
lost. You have memories of feeling helpless or hopeless, of

hating or failing. Your memory of not being loved, or your memory of being loved too much."

I looked over at my mother one last time. She was still crying, only now she couldn't look at me as she did it.

"So I am standing here to remind you all of this one fact: your memory has but one purpose — to help you understand. It doesn't exist to be dwelled on or to control you, or to paralyze you, skipping like a scratched CD, never allowing you to move past eight, past twelve, past sixteen. It's a key. And if you use the key correctly, it can help you move forward, make decisions, find peace and happiness in tomorrow so you can continue to make more memories, completely new memories, great memories. You are eighteen for one short year of your life and then, like all the rest of your years, it will become a memory.

"So. I hope you've made it a good one. I hope you will meet tomorrow with the attitude that you can do whatever your heart desires. Be sad, Antonia. Be afraid, Sonny. Be angry down to the bone, Javen. Just know that it's not all you ever have to be. Don't let those things define you. Be like my Papá who used his memory as fuel for his dreams.

"I use my memory of fishing with my father to remind me of how fortunate I am...fortunate that he didn't share the same fate as his brother. It also reminds me not to take tomorrow for granted, to put off your dreams for later, seeing as how later isn't a promise.

"In closing, I would like to ask for some favors before I leave all of you:

"To my Papá: Remember that you already have everything you need to make your dreams come true. You didn't need your brother and you don't need me. You don't have to wait for anyone's smarts to realize them.

"To mí Mama: Remember to save me a spot at the dinner table. I'll miss your albóndigas, but not half as much as I'll miss you.

"To Ramona: Remember to be a good girl. I'll be checking in on you.

"To my boys: Remember to take care of each other. And if you ever were my friends, you'll take care of our girl.

"Lastly, to Antonia: Recuerde que siempre estoy contigo.

"To the rest of you: Thanks for listening."

Even though I had read his words beforehand, it wasn't until I was up there, on the podium in front of what felt like the whole world, that I really heard them and realized that I would never see him again. He would never go to Texas A&M. He would never hold his girl again. He was gone, and the pain was awful.

Chapter 22
Antonia's Story

The day before graduation, I had the last of my infamous dreams: In the dream, I wore my favorite sweater, the one that's faded yellow, like Italian lemon ice, the one with the holes in the elbows and my left shoulder blade. I rode up to Spring Canyon in the late afternoon to watch a rainstorm descending on the desert basin. I was with my aunt Alicia. She'd never been here before, so I took great pleasure in pointing out the Needle's Eye, the yellow poppies in full bloom, the Persian ibex mountain goats climbing the jagged slopes of the Florida Mountains. I was in a dream, and in my dream I could be just as knowledgeable as Joey if I wanted to.

We parked and sat on the hood of the Suvee, sharing a bag of licorice. They were her favorites, too. She still couldn't talk to me, but speech wasn't necessary in this dream. I knew that I was forgiven for the way I had treated her the last time we'd met. I also knew that she was more concerned about receiving my forgiveness — for the gun, for bringing it into a home with small children, for putting it within a three-year-old's reach, and for leaving me alone in the room with it for even two seconds. She said these things without saying them. And I said *I forgive you* just as soundly. She was free. We both were.

Still, she knew why she'd been invited here. And I got the final answer I needed. The anonymous letter sent to Mom. She just smiled, and I knew it was her. She also told me that the old man and the old lady who always visited me in my dreams, those were my grandparents. I wish I had gotten to know them before they passed away. But then again, how many people get regular visits by their deceased grandparents? I *had* gotten to know them...in my sleep.

Aunt Alicia promised to be at my graduation. And she didn't lie. I felt her. I also felt Stacia, the hippie guy, but most of all, Joey. How could he not be there? It was his night. His words to me at the end of his speech "Remember that I am always with you," helped fill the emptiness in my heart.

After it was all over, I fought through the crowd and made my way to Mr. Diaz.

"Congratulations, mi'ja," he said.

"Thank you, Mr. Diaz." Looking into the sad eyes of my best friend's father, I didn't feel much like being congratulated.

"Would you do something for me, mi'jita?"

The last time someone asked me that question, I was left feeling tricked. But there was no way I could deny Mr. Diaz a favor, especially tonight.

"Anything. Anything for you, Mr. Diaz."

He fought back tears before finally speaking. "Please, call me Papá."

I took off my maroon cap and hugged him, glad that I'd let my heart answer instead of my head. It was a request that I was more than happy to oblige.

* * *

When I got back to the Suvee, I took off my gown and shoved it into my backpack. As I took off my heels to replace them with sneakers, someone tapped me on the shoulder. I turned around to find my mom, Madrid and Jewel standing there with an older man, someone who looked....

Before I finished the thought, he smiled at me and I knew. There was no question as to how to refer to *this* man.

"Dad?"

He nodded. "Beautiful Antonia." He said the words so unlike someone who hadn't seen me since I was a baby suffering from appendicitis.

"I can't believe you found us."

"I always knew where you were, Kiddo. I only stayed away because my heart kept insisting that it wasn't the right time. But how could I miss today? So, ready or not, here I am."

He was right to have stayed away. And right to have come when he did. We hugged one another tightly. He felt just the way I imagined he would — familiar. And yet he smelled new, like the interior of my graduation present, like California, like hope.

"I'm absolutely ready," I said.

When we finally broke apart, he reached into Jewel's handbag and pulled out a journal. *My journal!*

"Where did you get that?" I asked.

"I ran into a man who said it belonged to you."

I opened it up to my last entry. In it, there was a note not in my writing. *What was lost has now been found. I will be in touch.*

"By any chance was he an old hippie with dreadlocks and a foreign accent?"

"You know that guy?"

I laughed.

He was born in Lisbon, Portugal on August 15th, 1195. At baptism, he was given the name Fernando. And at the age of 25, the Franciscan Order gave him the name Anthony. On Friday the 13th of June, 1231, he died at the age of 36. Thirty two years later, his tomb was opened so his remains could be transferred to a sanctuary built in his honor. What was found when it was opened remains a mystery. His tongue had outlasted his body, remaining as fresh and ruddy as a living person's. It was proclaimed that the tongue of San Antonio lived on because it never ceased to praise God.

He held baby Jesus over twelve hundred years after he had been born. He approached a tiger in human form and reproached him for his sins. My saint, like Jesus, healed the sick and even raised the dead. He is famous for finding things that are lost. Over the years he was kind enough to help me find my keys, my checkbook, my driver's license and my dog. And on one beautiful and melancholic May morning, he came to my rescue. Mine. He'd rescued insignificant, selfish little me. Why he came as a hippie hitchhiker, I may never know. And why he did what he did for my sake is something that in all my life I will never be able to fathom. How was I so lucky? Why was I so blessed? Saying thank you could never have been enough. I had to show him I was thankful. And I would.

"He's a friend of mine," I answered. "But, you know, he was wrong. This actually belongs to you." My dad looked understandably puzzled.

"Thanks to Madrid, I had a place to write to you over the last few years. Open it. You'll see your name at the top of every entry." I handed it back to this man with eyes just like mine, only more tired, perfectly broken-in, like my horse or Joey's jeans.

Just before graduation, we'd packed our bags, gassed up the Suvee and prepared to hit I-10 to California right afterwards. Sonny was so kind. He'd taken the Suvee and cleaned it up. I think he needed to see the blood. See the last and blatant evidence of Joey's death. I let him clean my Suvee because I hoped that it would help him to deal with his own demons when they'd arise.

Now, the only thing to remind us of Joey's ever-presence was the standard wooden rosary given to all us Confirmation candidates that had hung on his rearview mirror. Now it hung on mine.

The guys were coming to California with us. They'd never been there before, and it was almost as if I hadn't either. I wanted to reacquaint myself with long, lost relatives, meet my mom's brother and my cousins that look "eerily" like Madrid. But I also wanted to ride that roller coaster on Mission Beach, watch the sun shimmer off the Pacific ripples, and drive by the house with the green cabinets and shag carpet. There wasn't anything left to remember. I was no longer like a rock-hound tourist searching for geodes on the hot desert hillsides. I was through looking for things that were scattered and hard to find. I just wanted a physical place to bury my nightmares once and for all.

Now, instead of one little Suvee driving west, we had two carloads going to San Diego, which included my grandmother, my father, my sister, and my best friends...my new and improved family. I drove with Javen, Jewel and the luggage. (I was behind the wheel this time.) Little did I know that Javen really hit it off with the ladies. Mom obviously loved him to pieces. As it turned out, so did Jewel.

Dad, Mom, Madrid, and her "new boyfriend" all traveled in the second car. Sonny and Madrid had become inseparable. Just like my mom and dad had. Madrid still had a lot of questions for our parents, a lot of accepting of her own to do. We had plenty of driving hours ahead of us for her to ask questions to her heart's content. And Sonny could always entertain them with stories of his grandmother's ghost.

As we drove down another desolate highway, I thought about Joey and Sonny and all their familial purity. Then I thought about Javen's parents, about how they'd gypped him of everything good and pure.

And then there was mine. Mom mixed goodness and purity together in a bottle with one part fear to produce an elixir called the New and Improved Truth. Madrid and I had drunk from it for many years. But the bottle was finally empty.

Would Joey's mother have done the same under the circumstances? Would Sonny's? Would I? How could I blame my mom for doing the best she knew how? She'd tried to sacrifice her own sanity for the sake of mine.

Don't get me wrong, I still have things I need to deal with as a full-fledged adult, but I can honestly look back over the last eighteen years and say that I had it good. I had silent vigils in heaven and here on earth, people watching my back, people keeping the light on for me amid all the other lights scattered like fairy dust across the western United States. I had it really good. Besides, Javen had prevailed at the opposite end of the spectrum, so there was no reason why I couldn't.

I looked over at his handsome face which was now just as calm as the Gila. I had almost forgotten that there was a dimple in his left cheek when he smiled. And that he hummed along to country tunes when he was happy. And that he opened doors for women! No, that one was definitely new.

Javen was my hand to hold through the funeral, my shoulder to cry on in the days that followed, my graduation partner when he didn't even want to be there. Like me, he had probably aged a whole ten years over the course of one week. But it wasn't just the passing of Joey that matured us and brought us closer. There was much more binding us together.

One puzzle remained unsolved. It concerned the letter I'd written, the one that Javen had been carrying around for so long. It was Joey's. How Javen had ended up with it, I may never know. Did I write the wrong name and address on the envelope? I didn't have Javen's physical address memorized, and he'd lived with Sonny at the time, anyway. It was bizarre. When he'd read me the words, I was shocked. Aside from the fact that he had the whole thing memorized, I couldn't believe it was in his possession and that he wholeheartedly felt it had been written for him.

Who knows, maybe it had been. I'm not sure how, but it did something for him. For us.

I think Joey would now have to agree that there aren't always explanations for everything. It's true, I finally got some answers with the help of my sisters, my saint, my dreams.... The Rosetta Stones of my life, if you will.

But I still choose to believe in magic and miracles, ghosts and God. I believe there are things that exist without explanation. I believe I am one of them. And maybe there are answers to everything, but I'm satisfied in knowing that, for now, God is the only keeper of them all.

Printed in the United States
140315LV00001B/1/P